BANGALORE CHRONICLES:
A KIDNAP

Bangalore Chronicles:
A Kidnap

Vinay Ramakrishna

Notion Press

Old No. 38, New No. 6

McNichols Road, Chetpet

Chennai - 600 031

First Published by Notion Press 2015

Copyright © Vinay Ramakrishna 2015

All Rights Reserved.

ISBN: 978-93-5206-296-6

To my parents and my sister

PREFACE

March 2013

"Sir, please help us out. We don't know what to do."

The austere silence from the authorities added to Vishu's helplessness. He sat in front of an Inspector who was engrossed in reading a complaint for what seemed like an eternity. Akhila, who sat beside him, desperately tried to calm him down. That he was anxious was to say the least of the raging turmoil he was experiencing. His friends had been missing for the last two days. His first encounter with a rude and dismissive officer earlier in the day made matters worse. The Inspector's office spoke eloquently of a sense of authority and power. A gilded plaque proudly proclaimed the officer to be "Aditya Shetty, Inspector". A pile of neatly organized files waited patiently in a corner for the officer to give them his time and attention. The Inspector himself was a picture of ease reclining in his black leather chair perusing the complaint.

"Yes, we are here to help you. Don't worry. Give me a minute while I finish reading this."

Momentarily, Vishu relaxed into his chair, as the Inspector seemed to understand his helplessness. The relaxation, however, did not last long. While the Inspector continued reading the case file, Vishu's gaze fell on a white board that hung behind the Inspector's chair. It had two columns – one mentioning the months and the other mentioning some numbers against each month. The puzzling numbers only made sense to him when he looked at the ominous title "Missing". The overwhelming number of people whose whereabouts could not be traced pushed his panic into overdrive. Disturbed by the statistics on the board, he looked away from them. The file cabinets stacked up against the wall drew his gaze and he noticed one of them had a "Missing" sign on it. He tore his gaze away from the cabinets and looked up to see a fan rotating at full speed. The creaking sound from the fan served only to aggravate his restlessness. Finally unable to bear the inaction, he closed his eyes and put his head down on the desk till the Inspector was done reading the complaint.

After reading the case file for a few more minutes, the Inspector put it on the table and leaned back contentedly in his chair.

'TRRING, TRRING!'

No sooner did the Inspector ring the bell on his desk than a constable entered the office. Vishu, startled by the sound, looked up to see what was going on.

"Bring three cups of tea!" The Inspector turned towards Vishu and asked, "You both drink tea, right?" After they nodded, he signaled to the constable to get the tea. "Get some biscuits as well." The constable marched away like a man on a mission.

The Inspector stared at Vishu for a few seconds before starting the conversation. It looked like he was trying to read Vishu's thoughts. The intensity in his eyes and cold body language made Vishu a little nervous.

"So? Three of your friends have been missing for the past two days. The last time you saw them was at college when you had an altercation with them. Is that right?"

"Yes, Sir. But I did not do any harm to them. Believe me, Sir. I am telling the truth."

"Vishu, I already said not to worry. I believe you."

"Thank you, Sir. I hope they are okay. The number of missing people in the last couple of months is making me very anxious." Vishu gestured at the board behind the Inspector's chair.

"What you are seeing is true. I won't deny it. We have been seeing a lot of these cases of late and we are working on it. However, we are not sure if they are interconnected or if they are random occurrences. I think it is too early to put your friends in this category."

There was a knock on the door and the constable entered bearing a tray of three steaming cups of tea. Beside the cups was a plate of neatly arranged biscuits. The aroma of tea enveloped the office and suddenly Vishu realized that he was very hungry. The Inspector took his cup from the tray and signaled to the other two to do the same. The Inspector took a sip and asked, "Tell me more about your friends. You have known them for quite some time right? What was the altercation about?"

"We met in college and the four of us were very close friends. We spent a lot of time together. Until the day before yesterday, everything seemed to go really well," Vishu began. He then reminisced about the good memories he had made with his friends.

ACKNOWLEDGEMENT

My sincere thanks to Vikram Krishnamurthy for being there from the initial stages of the book and reviewing it umpteen number of times. I am also grateful to Prajna Shetty for her valuable comments on each of the chapters.

I would like to extend my gratitude to my editor friend, Amulya Prabhakar for polishing the manuscript and getting the first edited version out.

Thanks to my friends, Vikram Krishnamurthy, Sujith Hosamane and Vijet Mahabaleshwar, from whom the characters are inspired.

I am grateful to all my friends who reviewed the final draft and gave me their valuable inputs on the flow and story. Thanks are due to those who have helped me in getting in touch with authors and publishers.

Special thanks go to Vivek Madhwaraj (for allowing me to use his name in the first chapter) and to my uncle Gopal Dindukurthi for allowing me to quote his saying in the first chapter.

I would like to thank everyone else who was involved in making this book reach its destination.

Last and the most important ones: I would like to say thanks to my parents and my sister for being pillars and supporting me in all my endeavors so far.

Chapter 1

October 2012

"Thank You!"

"Thank you, ladies and gentlemen. My sincere thanks to the honorary President of Dootha College of Engineering (DCE), to all the dignitaries, to the parents and to the students present here. I am greatly honored to be a part of this commencement ceremony.

I would like to start by thanking the most important people in my life. They have held my hand since the very beginning, helping me with problems that I face every day, guiding me to the path of success and making great sacrifices just for my welfare. They are my parents. If you are sitting here at the convocation ceremony, then a large part of the credit goes to your parents. Today is a very special day for your parents. Their dreams for you have come true and their sacrifices have paid off. There is no limit to the happiness they must be feeling seeing their sons and daughters graduate. Please take a moment to thank your parents, the architects of your life. Whenever I see a young batch of students in graduation gowns, it reminds me of my commencement ceremony. This may seem clichéd. But believe me, it truly is an unforgettable moment in life. It has been 15 years now, but the image is crystal clear in my mind. On the day of my commencement ceremony, I wore a black gown and a yellow hood, the color representing the computer science branch. The honorary guest was an alumnus of DCE, Mr. Vivek Madhwaraj, a Nobel Peace Laureate, an innovator, a businessman and a genius. His work for the welfare of orphaned kids is commendable. His speech was one of the best I have heard till date. At that very moment, I started dreaming about me giving a convocation speech to graduating students.

I have rehearsed these lines many a time in my dreams. All that effort, however, is not helping me today with the speech. It might be the aura of the excellence sitting around me that is making me nervous. On the day of my commencement, I had several questions in my mind. Why was Mr. Vivek Madhwaraj selected as the guest speaker? Was he the best student of his batch? If not, then why weren't the better ones invited?

Frankly, even to this day, I do not have answers to those questions. I don't even know why I was selected as the guest speaker for today. I was clearly not the best student of my batch. But one thing was clear to me. Outside of college, it is not only the marks and grades but also your ability to use the knowledge for the greater good that makes you unique. I had a lot of dreams and ideas to make our world a better place to live in. But I had no idea where to start. I realized that I have to start with smaller targets before I can think of doing something big for society. I decided to start by providing support to orphaned children. The preparation towards this goal took over a year to start and a further two years to reach fruition. This first step later grew to providing better education and facilities to the under privileged over a period of ten years. My enthusiasm and vigor never waned through all my dreams and I still chase dreams with the same attitude. In my journey of dreams and fulfilling them,

I was granted several opportunities to meet and learn from the best teacher in my life. I am sure all of us have met this teacher at least once so far.

And that teacher is 'Failure'.

Yes, you heard right! Failure has been the best teacher in my life. Failure is curt, unemotional, untimely and brutally honest. But it is always right. Unlike Success, it does not hide your weaknesses. It points to the areas where you need to work on and like any other teacher; it puts forth a test in front of you – 'A Test of Attitude'. To prove your mettle; to raise your bars; to stay more focused; to work even harder; to achieve higher excellence. Yes, Failure teaches you all these.

As the saying goes, Success is a bastard as it has many fathers, and Failure is an orphan, with no takers. Don't shy away from trying out new things fearing Failure. Embrace it. In the long run, Failure will teach you to conquer life itself.

Today, I would like to say a few words about Hernán Cortés, who was one of the Spanish conquistadors. He is remembered for his victory against the Aztec. The Aztec army was so huge that the Spanish were clearly outnumbered. Cortés had arrived with just 11 ships for the war. But there was one thing he did that showed his attitude towards his goals. He scuttled all his ships. He wanted to give a clear signal to his army that retreat was not just unacceptable but impossible.

It portrayed that he believed in his dream and would go to any extent to fulfill it even if the dream seemed difficult to achieve. He used clever tactics in the war that in combination with native allies and epidemics of disease brought about the fall of the mighty Aztec empire. Dreams are fuel for life, fuel for success and fuel for excellence.

As my uncle puts it, 'You have learned how to learn things'. The actual learning begins now when you go out into the industry. Education not only gives knowledge, but also gives perspective. Make use of that perspective to see what is right for your career. For most people, need takes higher precedence than passion. Stop working for the need. Work for the passion. It will take you places. These words by William Ernest Henley have inspired me in all aspects of life and I hope that it will inspire you as well. '*I am the master of my fate. I am the captain of my soul*' With that I will conclude my speech, my best wishes to the graduating students. Let your journey be filled with dreams and let each one of them come true. Thank you!"

The audience erupted into thunderous applause when Mr. Vishwas Rana, the guest speaker for the convocation concluded his speech. The stadium, named after Sir M Visvesvaraya, where the commencement was proceeding, was packed with students and their families. This stadium was constructed at DCE to commemorate the 150ᵗʰ Birth Anniversary of Sir M Visvesvaraya, an '*Architect of many cities*' in India. The guest speech was followed by a series of small speeches and as a grand finale; the President announced the department name and officially conferred the degree to the students. The students of the respective department, once they heard it, threw their caps up in the air with joy and enthusiasm. Many stood up on chairs to catch their caps. The energy in the stadium was contagious. The stadium had transformed into a completely different environment where happiness engulfed everybody. It seemed like a crowded carnival ground. The dignitaries on the podium had formed small groups and were enjoying their moment by sharing the various experiences they had with the students, during their tenure at DCE. At this time, the President realized that the guest speaker, Vishwas Rana, was nowhere to be seen among the dignitaries. The President finally noticed him standing in one corner of the podium and just relishing the moment gazing at the students and families. The President approached him and noticed that he had tears in his eyes and that he was deeply moved by the emotions overflowing in the stadium. The President patted his back and praised him for his inspirational speech.

❖❖❖❖

The tapping on Vishu's shoulder continued, jolting him from his reverie. Vishu was stunned to find that he was sitting in the last bench in the classroom. It took him a few seconds to realize that he had fallen asleep in the class. He saw his friends, Srini and Sivu sitting beside him. Avi was sitting in front of him. Srini was insistently tapping his shoulder and trying to wake him up.

"Get up! Get up!"

The Professor, Ravi Nagraj shouted, "I told you to stand up." He was standing on the dais in front of the classroom from where he could see every student in the classroom that comfortably seated over a hundred students. The Professor was lecturing on the course "Computer Concepts and C programming". This was the only course related to the field of computer science for all first year students. Professor Ravi Nagraj was stout, no taller than five feet two, wearing a golf cap, glasses with a square frame and a tie at all times. He stood on the dais for a few seconds without saying a word, staring at a stunned Vishu who had stood up by then and was facing him. With a gruff, impatient tone he asked, "Now answer me, what are the different types of storage classes in C?"

Vishu could barely process the question in his mind let alone answer it. He tried hard to remember anything related to the storage classes in C. He recollected that he had referred to a few books about storage classes to complete a lab assignment recently. Unfortunately, he couldn't remember the answer. He could feel every eye in the classroom staring at him. He felt like his mind had shrunk and could no longer process any question.

Vishu started to mumble, "Aaah… storage classes… types in C language…" Professor waited, patiently listening to Vishu's mumbling. Then he said he had a simpler question to ask.

"At least tell me, who is the father of 'C'?"

Vishu started wondering how this was a simpler question. Does anyone really need to know the founder or the inventor of what they are learning? Does it mean that people know about the inventors of everything that they work in or of the products that they use on a day-to-day basis? How many people know that a person named John Loud first patented the ballpoint pen in the year 1888 that we use so regularly? Or how many know that Dr. Martin Cooper of Motorola tested the first cell phone successfully in 1973? There are millions of people who use both products without knowing about the inventors or the so-called fathers of the products. Vishu stood with his head bowed, trying to see if he could find the answer to the question miraculously on the table somewhere. He could not recollect anything about the founder of C. At that moment his mind was like a clean slate, yet to be used. In the glare of the unwanted spotlight, what his classmates might be thinking about him overwhelmed him. He wanted to get away from the spotlight as soon as possible. The Professor was angry with

Vishu as he was not aware of a seemingly simple question. He started yelling, "You are leaving the classroom if I see such a thing happening again during my lecture. This is my final warning!"

Vishu was so desperate to get away from the spotlight that he heard only the first few words spoken by his Professor and assumed that he was being asked to leave the classroom. He quickly packed his bag and did not even wait for the Professor to finish. He just stormed out of the classroom taking everyone, including the Professor, by surprise. He climbed down two floors and walked outside the Computer Science department to the lawn in the front. He walked towards the parking lot adjacent to the admissions office. Since he was no longer the center of attention, he began thinking cogently about the two questions that stumped him in the classroom. He analyzed the first question. 'What are the different types of storage classes in C?' and in no time, he remembered three out of four types of storage classes, *auto*, *static* and *register*. They referred to the programming language C and were indicators of where the variables reside within a program. With a little more thought underway, he recollected even the final type of storage class as being *extern*. As he entered the parking lot that was lined up with bikes, he mulled over the second question. He had known the answer to the question before. After a few minutes of thinking while still walking in the parking lot, he remembered when he had first heard about the father of C.

"Now it is Team Unleashed's turn! Are you guys ready? The question goes like this", a female host with her pleasant voice, asked the question in the first round of the Tech quiz, organized as part of the Computer Science department fest at Dootha College of Engineering.

"Identify the person related to Computer Science field. His first and the last name are formed by the first name of two famous comic strips characters," asked the host.

One of the team members of Team Unleashed said, "Next clue, please."

"You will be now playing for 10 points instead of 15 points. Second clue: He is known as father of C", indicated the host.

"Dennis Ritchie," both the team members of Team Unleashed blurted out.

"That is absolutely correct. Dennis Ritchie is known as the father of C. Dennis is the name of the comic character in Dennis the Menace and Ritchie is from the comic strip Richie Rich. Good job team," said the host.

After remembering this incident, it hit Vishu that he had borrowed a book from his senior "The C programming Language" authored by Kernighan and Ritchie. The author Ritchie was Dennis Ritchie himself. Vishu had reached the end of the parking lot by then. He kicked a small stone in an effort to vent his anger at not being able to recollect the answers in class. The stone hit a pillar and made a sharp noise jolting him out of his reverie. He just stood there staring at the board mounted on the pillar. The board was a wooden plank proclaiming in bold lettering "Dootha College of Engineering, Est. 1947". The plank and the words both reminded Vishu of an era long lost in the sands of time. Vishu was still staring at the board when the college bell rang, making a shrill noise. The old fashioned bell mounted above the admissions office rang everyday signaling the end of classes. Vishu walked a little further from the board and saw the old soiled banner tied to a tree he had noticed that morning. It was a banner of a previous year's commencement ceremony. The guest speaker was Vivek Madhwaraj. He was surprised that a name he had read in passing had become a central figure of his dream. He walked ahead to a huge tree in the center of the pathway with stone seating below the tree. The place had stone benches all around it for students to sit and chat under the shade. This place affectionately known as "The Katte" was one of the popular hangout spots in the college for Vishu and his friends. Vishu sat on one of the benches and he saw his three close friends, Sivu, Srini and Avi walking towards him.

As they sat next to Vishu, Sivu started the conversation. "You did not have to leave the classroom. The Professor was just warning you. Why did you leave?"

Vishu was taken by surprise. "I heard him say leave the classroom and so I came out. What was he saying by the way?"

Srini started to giggle and said, "You did not listen to the full thing, did you? He was just warning you."

"Were you not able to recollect those two answers?" questioned Sivu.

"I knew the answers for both the questions that the Professor asked."

"Then what happened over there? Why were you stammering like a confused kid?" asked Avi.

Vishu putting his head down in frustration and said, "I don't know why I was stammering. I wasn't able to think clearly with everyone staring at me. I have no idea what happens to me in public."

CHAPTER 2

The next morning, the sun had risen a couple of hours ago and yet there was hardly any sunshine because of the fog, so characteristic of Bangalore weather. Blessed by a vast number of trees, the city enjoys a pleasant weather throughout the year. Numerous parks and gardens in the city had earned it the title "Garden City", much before the Indian Independence. The outsiders often cribbed about the foggy weather, complaining that it made them lazy and gloomy but the residents of the city completely relished this type of weather, typically with a cup of piping hot coffee. For the same reason of enjoying a cup of coffee in this weather, Srini forced the other three guys to miss the first lecture of the day. They grabbed a coffee from one of the kiosks within the campus and walked to the Katte to savor it. They usually discussed random topics when they sat on the Katte to kill time. Today's topic was cricket and to be more specific, the legend Rahul Dravid's aka "The Wall's" retirement.

"The Wall is retiring. Test matches without him will be boring!" exclaimed Srini.

Vishu said, "I feel he was over shadowed by Sachin Tendulkar. If not for that guy, he would have been the greatest player in Indian history." Vishu hardly knew that he had asked for trouble by striking the wrong chord at that time. Avi was looking to vent his anger and when his God 'Sachin Tendulkar' was dragged into the discussion, there was no stopping him.

"You cannot compare two individuals that way. I agree that Dravid is a very good player but Tendulkar is in a different league altogether. A league of his own, which no other player can imagine coming anywhere close to," argued Avi.

Sivu jumped into the conversation. "What Vishu meant was that Dravid did not get due credits for his achievements. He was never front-page news fodder, like Tendulkar."

"That is mainly because of Tendulkar's records and achievements. A person who has played for more than two decades for India deserves more. No human has done it till now except for Tendulkar and that's why he is aptly known as the God among his fans across the world," snapped Avi.

Vishu tried to explain his view. "Let's just calm down and think for a moment. If Tendulkar was not around, who else do you think would have been the greatest player in the Indian history?"

"There are no Ifs and Buts in the world of cricket. That is the beauty of the game."

"I read this somewhere. At night, even 'God' is behind the 'Wall'," giggled Srini.

Avi got annoyed and blurted, "Cut the crap dude. That's not even funny." Srini's attempt at pacifying his enraged friends did not work out well. Avi was in no mood to listen to anyone. By then, Vishu had lost his patience trying to get his friends to see his perspective. He thought it was fruitless staying on the same topic. He started looking around and saw other students passing by. But Sivu was persistent and continued to debate, which seemed to go nowhere.

"You need to think with an unbiased mind. You cannot undermine Dravid's accomplishments."

"I am not! In fact, I am happy for his accomplishments. All I am saying is that Tendulkar is in a different league and you need to stop comparing him with anyone else."

Srini tried to step in again and restore peace. "Okay fine. Tendulkar and Dravid are in two different leagues. Will you stop now? Shall we change the topic?"

Avi nodded and mumbled, "You tell them to stop arguing."

By now, Vishu had stopped listening to the conversation. His attention was on a girl who had entered the parking lot and found a spot to park her scooter in. It was Akhila Nayak, also a first year student in the Information Technology department and Vishu knew her from day one at DCE. Today, she was wearing a mauve colored hoodie with blue jeans and black sandals. She had worn purple earrings and nail polish to match the color of the hoodie. She wore her long straightened hair loose, cascading in waves that reached just beyond her shoulder. She shouldered a bag that she took out from the scooter case and was toying with her hair in the mirror before she started walking.

"Hey Akhila! Stop! Wait for me." Vishu jumped up from the katte and walked toward her. She turned around saw him coming and stood by the scooter waiting for him.

"Hi Vishu!" They smiled and shook hands.

"How are you? Long time!"

"I am fine. Yeah! Long time since we last met. Where are you these days?" asked Akhila.

"Last week I was busy with my course work. By the way, I saw you yesterday in parking lot but you left before I could reach you."

"Oh? Yeah, I was in a hurry yesterday and left immediately after the classes. Sorry, I didn't notice you."

"That's fine. I was just returning from the cafeteria."

Both of them stood there for a few moments without speaking. Despite the awkward silence, they were smiling hesitantly at each other. Vishu thought he saw a spark in her eyes when she smiled at him. He had a lot of things to tell her, but he wasn't able open his mouth. He wanted to ask her out and spend more time with her in a café or someplace nearby. The fear of rejection however rendered him speechless. His thoughts had trailed off when he heard his name being called in chorus from behind. It was his friends calling his name continuously, not willing to miss any opportunity for teasing him.

"Alright then. I will leave. Bye," she said.

"Bye!" Vishu turned around as she headed to her department and walked to the Katte. "Idiots! You guys didn't allow me to talk to her."

"We were just calling out your name. Sorry, were we interrupting something?" quipped Avi.

Srini sat next to Vishu and said, "You need to ask her out. You have been mooning over her since day one at college and you hardly talk to her. It is obvious that she likes you too."

"Oh yeah! I remember the first day of college." Vishu recollected the thrills and spills of the first day at Dootha College of Engineering.

❖

DAY ONE AT DOOTHA COLLEGE OF ENGINEERING

The bell at DCE rang indicating 9:00 AM in the morning. It was the first day of engineering for a new batch of students. They started pouring in from all directions. The loud sound from the antique bell ended up making everyone move faster in an effort to get to his or her classes on time. The Principal's car, with the sticker "Principal of DCE" on the rear windshield, came to a screeching halt in front of his office indicating his punctuality. The hurried footsteps of students at the entrance of the campus had an almost rhythmic tune. Sprinklers in the garden in front of the Tata Auditorium, near the entrance of DCE, were revolving and spraying water to the lush lawn. The noise that the revolving sprinklers made gelled with the ambient sound forming a rhythm. The security guard at the gate added his share of sound by blowing his whistle every now and then as the vehicles entered the campus.

Vishwas Rana alias Vishu was a little over five-and-half feet tall and he had a skinny build. This along with his unkempt hair made him look younger and even though he was in his college, he could easily pass off as a high school kid. He belonged to a place called Kittur near HD Kote about 50 kilometres from Mysore. Since his school days he had always fared well at academics. His choice of Computer Science as a major had come as a surprise to his parents and those who knew him. Having done exceedingly well in Electronics in high school, everyone had assumed that he would be pursuing a career majoring in that. Despite having had an option to go to other colleges where career opportunities were significantly larger, he had chosen DCE. His wish to be a part of a college like DCE, where free will and independence was promoted, had prompted him to consider an alternate major. At present, he was sitting on the steps of the open-air theater, next to the auditorium, and gazing at the DCE board that was hung at a distance. He was trying to assimilate the fact that he had opted to join the Computer Science stream in the Engineering at DCE. He was shaken out of his reverie by the insistent honking of a food truck at the entrance of the gate. He saw a guy wearing earphones standing in the center of the driveway with both his hands stretched wide open and looking at the sky. It looked as if he was in a trance, praying to God looking up. Vishu smiled thinking that it was crazy to stand in the middle of the entrance in that manner blocking the vehicles. The guy finally gave way to the honking trunk to pass.

As Vishu continued to look, the guy with earphones bumped into a tall, lean guy with well-groomed hair who was standing by the side of the road and chatting with few people. He said something to the tall guy that Vishu could not figure out. The guy with the earphones had dropped his wallet during the collision. As Vishu was getting up to retrieve the wallet, he saw another student had picked up the wallet and was returning it. Instantly, Vishu yelled "Srini" and waved to the student who returned the wallet. Srini turned around and saw Vishu standing on the steps of the open-air theater. He waved back at Vishu and started walking towards the steps.

◄◙◆◘►

Srinavas Wah aka Srini was around six feet tall and had broad shoulders. He was a simple and smart guy, but one of the shy ones. He rarely put forth his view in classroom discussions, although he was equally active in non-classroom conversations. Although he was a foodie, he never seemed to put on weight and had always maintained good physique. When it came to strenuous work such as workouts, trekking or outdoor games, he preferred staying away from them. He believed in having fun by doing things that did not consume a lot of energy. He was practical and took decisions only after giving them ample thought. He was born and brought up in Bangalore. On the first day of college, Srini had woken up early and reached the campus by 8:30 AM. He walked around the campus at an excited pace. He saw the cafeteria, the stone benches under the tree near the parking lot, the open-air theater in front of the TATA auditorium and also the colossal Sir M Visvesvaraya stadium. He visited the computer science block that was soon to become his block for the next four years. As the bell in the campus struck indicating 9:00 AM, Srini started walking towards the admissions office, near the entrance of the college. At that moment, the Principal's car came to a stop in front of the admissions office building, which also contained his office.

He stood near the admissions office building and started looking around. Few people were already sitting in the open-air theater. One of them, a lean guy, was staring intently at the DCE board. Amused by that, Srini slowly turned his attention towards the entrance of the college. He saw many students entering and one of them in particular caught his attention. He seemed extremely excited, looking around with wondrous eyes and a pair of earphones jammed into his ears. As Srini continued watching him he came to a sudden stop at the entrance, stretched out both his arms and looked up towards the sky. He was blocking the way and a truck was creeping in behind him. He tried waving and grabbing the attention of the guy with earphones, but to no avail. The truck driver stopped the vehicle a few meters away from the guy with earphones and started honking. Annoyed by the noise, he stared at the driver and stepped aside allowing the truck to pass. As he started walking inside, he bumped into another tall guy who was busy chatting with other students. All this while, Srini was watching him and noticed that the guy with earphones had dropped his wallet. He picked and returned it to that guy. At the same moment, someone from behind started calling out Srini's name. He turned around to see a lean guy with unkempt hair standing in the open-air theater and waving his hand. He realized that this was the same guy who had been staring at the DCE board a while ago. The guy was none other than Vishwas, a friend of Srini's close pal. They had met on a couple of occasions earlier. Srini waved back and started walking towards him.

Vishu shook hands and said, "Hi! Long time. How are you?"

"Hi Vishu! Yeah, long time since we met. I am good. How about you?"

"Never been better. Excited to be here and to become a part of this prestigious college. I still feel like it is all a dream."

"Very true. If I have got it right, then you must be part of Computer Science Dept too correct?"

Beaming with joy, Vishu replied, "Yep. I am."

"Then we will be classmates for the next four years. Wonderful!"

"Shall we check out the campus? I was waiting for some company."

"Of course. I already saw couple of places in the morning. I visited the computer science department. It is a big building with huge classrooms and labs with rows of computers. I saw a board outside the lab that mentioned free Internet for students. That is so cool. I also saw the colossal stadium at other end of the college. It has a seating capacity of a few thousand at the least!"

"Oh yeah. Let's check out the stadium first," Vishu said excitedly. They started walking towards the stadium. They had to pass through the parking lot and then the stone benches under the tree at the end of the parking lot.

Srini asked, "When did you reach Bangalore? I remember vaguely that you are from a place called Kittur, aren't you?"

Vishu nodded and answered, "Yup. I came to Bangalore a week ago. I got accommodation in Basavangudi area itself. I did not opt for the dorm facility at the hostel."

"That's great. More freedom if you live outside. I opted to live in the dorm for this year."

Vishu was about to say something but someone from behind interrupted him. Both of them turned to see a group of senior students calling out to them. They were sitting on the stone benches, more famously known as the "Katte". Vishu turned to see two other guys who were already standing in front of the seniors. Instantly, he recognized one of them as the guy with earphones he had seen earlier. But he could not place the other guy. There were seniors sitting on the Katte. They had been stopping the juniors and ragging them. One of the seniors asked, "Introduce yourself. Tell us your name and where you are from."

Srini was the first one to speak, "I am Srinivas. I am from Bangalore."

Vishu was next. He mumbled his name that was heard by no one. The senior, visibly annoyed, rudely said, "Speak up! No one is able to understand anything!" Vishu said, "My name is Vishwas Rana and I am from Kittur."

The guy with the earphones was next. He spoke confidently. "I am Avinash and I am from Yellapur. It is a place in Uttar Kannada District!" He beamed with enthusiasm and excitement at being able to represent his hometown.

⋯⋯◆⋯⋯

Avinash Swar, in short Avi, was around 5 feet and 6 inches tall and a lean guy. He was a quick-witted person, always ready with witty repartees. He was known for his poems and jokes. He was an ardent follower of music and idolized A. R. Rahman, one of the living legends in the Indian music industry. He had the habit of listening to few hours of music everyday and that included the time he spent inside the classrooms as well. He was born and brought up in a town called Yellapur and he was very excited to be part a big city and a prestigious college. On the first day at DCE, Avi got ready early in the morning to leave for college. He had a sleepless night, the excitement of the opening day of college keeping him up all night. He walked to the college, enjoying the pleasant weather with soothing music. With his earphones plugged in to an iPod and his favorite artist A.R. Rahman's song playing, his strut resembled that of an excited teenager going to a concert. It was a good fifteen-minute walk to the campus from the hostel dorm, but far from complaining, it looked as though he was enjoying the walk. Avi reached college around 9:00 AM. The striking sound of the bell from DCE was audible even from outside. As he neared the college gate, he saw a car pass by him and seeing the sticker behind it, he figured it was the college Principal who had just driven in. Just the fact that he was in the college was thrilling and his excitement knew no bounds. He felt a sense of accomplishment, as making it into one of the top engineering colleges of the state was no mean feat.

He stood at the entrance of the gate and took a moment to soak in the feeling. Spreading his hands wide, he closed his eyes and turned his head to the skies in appreciation. The cool breeze and the music from the pod seemed to dramatize the moment. He was rooted to the spot in the posture, blind to the horde of people passing by him. His moment of peace was shattered by the honk of a truck behind him. He just noticed that he was actually blocking the entrance of the college. But he was annoyed by the fact that the noise disturbed his moment of elation. The honking continued and after a few seconds, Avi gave the driver a nasty look before moving to the side. As he entered the college, he noticed an open-air theater and the garden on his right. Behind the garden, he could see the auditorium. On his left, he saw the admissions office building and also saw the Principal's car parked in front of the building. Few more steps ahead, he was so engrossed in noticing buildings and things around that he did not see a couple of people standing right in his way. He bumped into a tall, lean guy with perfectly groomed hair who was talking to two other people in the group.

Avi said, "Oh, I am sorry!" The tall guy shrugged and said, "No worries."

A couple of steps ahead, after he thought that the tall guy could not hear, Avi sarcastically mumbled to himself,

"Moron! Blocking the walkway" and continued walking. He walked further looking around the campus and awed by the things around him. Someone from behind shouted, "Excuse me! Hello!"

Avi turned around to see a well-built guy waving and walking towards him with a wallet in the guy's hand. He realized that he had dropped his wallet in the commotion earlier. Thanking the well-built guy, Avi continued further into the college. He approached an intersection and stood there staring at the signboard placed near it. The board indicated that the departments and classroom blocks were on his right and it said the Sir M Visvesvaraya stadium, parking lot and the cafeteria were on his left. He contemplated where to go for a few seconds before deciding to head towards the cafeteria. He entered the parking lot first, enjoying the music that was still playing from his iPod. He could see a group of students sitting on the stone bench at the end of the parking lot. He continued walking ahead but one of the students from the group waved his hand and asked Avi to come to them. Avi immediately realized that they were the seniors who wanted to rag him. He was thrilled at being picked for ragging because he had only heard of it, but never been a part of it. He got this opportunity now to see and experience it firsthand. He went and stood there in front of the group and was waiting for them to say something. The group was busy looking for a few more new students before they could start ragging. Avi stood there watching them silently. In a matter of few minutes, three other guys were called and made to stand in line next to him. When the seniors asked for an introduction, Avi spoke after the other two guys next to him. Once he was done, he turned towards the tall, lean guy with well-combed hair who was standing beside him who went next.

Sivu came forward and nonchalantly said, "I am Siva Sharan and I am from Shimoga."

⊷⊃◆⊂⊶

Siva Sharan W, aka Sivu, was around 6 feet and 1 inch, slim and fair. He was obsessed with his hair and at every available opportunity he ran a comb through it. It was not surprising that he carried a comb in his bag all the time. He was a smart guy and spoke English very well. He could strike up a conversation with anyone and as a result, he maintained a good rapport with his batch mates, including the girls. He had a habit of saying contextual proverbs in Kannada, the official language of the state of Karnataka. He had relocated to Bangalore from a place called Shimoga a month before. He had also bought a non-geared scooter before the college opened.

On the first day, Sivu reached the college on his scooter. He wore a helmet that resembled the one worn by civil engineers or architects at their work site, just covering the head, having no visor and totally exposing the ears and jaws. Being a tall guy, the scooter and the helmet did not go well with his physique. He entered the college early in the morning and decided to go around the campus on his scooter. He quickly finished his tour of DCE on his scooter without stopping anywhere. He looked at his watch and it was ten minutes to 9:00 am. He had to hurry up as he had promised to meet couple of the seniors in front of the admissions office at 9:00 AM. They belonged to the second year at DCE and he had got their contacts from one of his friends. He entered the parking lot to drop off his scooter. The students were walking in the parking lot making it difficult for Sivu to maneuver his scooter into an empty slot. He lost his patience when he was not able to go ahead any further. He honked at a well-built guy in front of him, who was walking slowly and enjoying the campus. He moved aside and apologized for blocking Sivu's way. Sivu went ahead and found an empty slot to park his vehicle. He started walking towards the admissions office building, which he had noticed earlier.

As the bell struck at nine, he was in front of the admissions office. He waited for some time for the seniors to arrive and noticed the Principal's car stopping near the admissions building. He turned around and saw the beautiful green garden and also noticed the noisy sprinklers busy watering the garden. He spotted the auditorium a little further away from the garden. He saw the open-air theater next to the auditorium and noticed that a few students were already sitting there. A guy staring at the DCE hoarding intently for a long time caught his attention and amused him. By then, two guys came from the entrance near admissions office and called his name aloud. They were the seniors whom Sivu was eagerly waiting to meet. After the formal handshakes and warm welcomes, the discussion went on about the DCE and the courses. Couple of minutes into their discussion, a shrill honking noise from the truck near the entrance gate, made Sivu turn around to watch what was happening over there. They continued talking about DCE and how the seniors had managed so far. Sivu was listening enthusiastically about his seniors' experiences. He was interrupted abruptly by a jolt. He looked up to see that a guy with earphones had bumped right into him. After exchanging apologies, the guy moved on mumbling something, which felt strange to Sivu. After realizing that this was the same guy who had blocked the college entrance a few seconds ago, Sivu thought, "Such an Idiot! He first blocks the entrance and now bumps into people randomly. On top of that he has earphones plugged in just to pose as if he is busy listening to music. A big show off!"

The guy with earphones was not finished apparently. He was receiving a wallet from another guy. Sivu recognized that guy who was returning the wallet was none other than the well-built guy who was blocking his way in the parking lot. Involuntarily, Sivu checked his pockets and found that his own wallet was missing. He remembered that he had taken it out from his scooter and assumed it might have fallen somewhere in the parking lot. He told the seniors that he had to get his wallet and they agreed to meet in the cafeteria, which was next to the parking lot, near the stone benches. Sivu hurriedly walked towards the parking lot to his scooter. He found his wallet lying beside the scooter. He put it back in his pocket carefully and started walking towards the cafeteria to meet the seniors. He passed the parking lot and was in front of the Katte. He saw the guy with earphones once again. Only this time, he was in front of a group of students, who were sitting on the Katte. Out of curiosity, he slowed down to see what was happening over there. One of the seniors from the group waved to Sivu and told him to come near them. Promptly, Sivu walked towards them and stood next to the guy with earphones. There were two others as well, whom Sivu recognized as the guy staring at the College Board and the other was the well-built guy who handed the wallet to the earphones guy.

Once all four names and places were told, the seniors started staring for a moment. The senior who had asked for introduction said, "Leave now. We are done here!" The four of them started walking away from the stone benches and entered the parking lot. Among the four, Avi was dejected. He wanted to see and experience ragging personally but that opportunity had slipped past him.

"Why did he tell us to leave?" questioned Avi. "What went wrong there?"

"I am curious too," replied Srini.

"Who cares? We do not have to do any of their stupid tasks in front of everyone anymore. Be happy for that," said Sivu. Vishu was walking on one side of the parking lot with his head down. He was not listening to their conversation.

"You were funny over there! Nice way to tackle the ragging. I am impressed." It was a pleasant voice of a girl. Vishu looked up and saw a girl standing by the scooter watching him. He was confused that someone was praising him when he was not even able to give his introduction right at the first time. He came to a halt in front of her while the others continued walking.

"Hi, I am Akhila!"

Akhila Nayak was born and brought up in Bangalore. She was an outstanding student right from the beginning of her school days. Her academics were really impressive except for the entrance exam to engineering courses. She fell ill and could not secure a good rank, in turn missing the opportunity to pursue her engineering in Computer Science. However, she was able to get the admission at DCE in the Information Technology stream of engineering. She was short - around 5 feet, long straightened hair, fair and looked very young. No one would have guessed her real age by looking at her face.

"Hi, my name is Vishu."

"I am a fresher too."

"Oh great. Which department?" Vishu asked.

"Information Technology. Yours?"

"Computer Science!"

"Oh! We have a geek here!" she teased with a smile.

Vishu ignored the comment. He asked, "Which place are you from?"

"I am from Bangalore. I was born and brought up here."

"Good. I am from Kittur, a town near Mysore." Vishu quickly ran out of topics to continue the conversation. He felt it better to end the conversation for now.

"Okay then. Nice talking to you. I will catch you later."

"Likewise. Bye." she said.

He went ahead and joined the other three guys who were waiting for him at the entrance of the parking lot. He had one unanswered question still. "Why did she say to me that I was funny over there? Was I?"

"Are you kidding me? You were not funny. She just wanted to start a conversation. This is how you initiate a conversation. I will teach you the tricks," snickered Sivu. Vishu agreed.

It had been more than four months since that day when the turn of events bought these four guys together and Vishu had grown closer to all the three guys. He used to hang around with them most of the time. As for Akhila Nayak, he used to meet her every now and then in college. His conversations with her were usually short, as Vishu would not know how to continue further and he would eventually end up wrapping it up soon.

Chapter 3

'Now let me give you a brief overview of the latest design of the engine. I will keep it as simple as possible so that you can easily grasp the idea. By the way, I am not from the mechanical engineering stream. So, please pardon me if I am not up to the mark. The USP of the engine is that it uses water instead of any other traditional fuels. The water used by the engine is recollected in the tank making it a "fill once and drive forever" design, thereby saving a lot of resources. Since there is no emission, this design is suited for betterment of the environment and for the reduction of air pollution. If successfully implemented, this design can be used in two-wheelers to begin with and later extended to all other vehicles after suitable modifications. Implementing this in our vehicles will ensure a much better tomorrow for the future generations. Let me get into the finer details of the engine. Do you see the tank at the top? That is where we fill in the water. The capacity of the tank is six liters. There are nozzles at the bottom of the tank, which form the outlet for the water. They have lids which open and close in accordance with the piston movement. These nozzles are pointing to the piston of the engine. There is a circular shaft within the tank with wide blades mounted on it. The shaft derives power from the battery to rotate which in turn rotates the blades. The engine design remains the same as that of a two-stroke diesel engine for the most part. The water leaving the engine is fed back into the upper water tank. Now, how many of you here would like to see the engine running on our roads?'

Many hands went up in the Tata auditorium at DCE where the Big Bang Day event was happening. The event happened every year at DCE and the purpose was to bring out innovative ideas from the students. A jury of professors picked the top five ideas that were funded and pursued in the lab as research. Vishwas Rana was on the stage demonstrating his idea of an engine that ran on water. He believed that an alternative source to fuel had to be figured out soon as using up all the available gasoline did not seem reasonable and everlasting anymore. He chose one of the most ubiquitous resources on the planet, water, and came up with an initial design that was later improvised by his friends in the mechanical department of DCE. Once the design was finalized, he built the engine and was ready with the prototype for the Big Bang Day event. He continued with his demonstration of the engine.

"Okay. Thank you for your response. Let me show how this engine works without any further delay. The shaft and the blades in the tank rotate by turning on the power. The rotating blades push down the water building pressure inside. Once the nozzles open up, water hits the piston with great force making the piston move forward. As the piston is pushed away, the nozzles close and hence the water stops leaving the tank. Once the piston returns, the nozzles open again. The opening and closing of the nozzles coordinate along with the piston movement, in turn causing the vehicle to move. This represents a two-stroke engine with an inlet stroke and an outlet stroke. The water leaving the engine is fed back to the tank as we can see here. I can assure you that there will be no wastage of water in this design and I can validate the point by showing you all the level of water in the tank. Here I put my fingers in the tank and I see the water at the brim of the tank. Wait a minute. But why is the water getting hotter inside? Holy cow!"

Vishu yanked his finger away and put it in his mouth to cool off. He was startled to get the taste of coffee from his fingers. He looked around and realized that he was in the cafeteria within the campus. His friends Sivu, Avi and Srini were sitting around him, laughing out loud. An hour ago, Vishu was in the classroom and professor Ashish Choudary was lecturing on a mechanical course. He was a tall, lean guy with mocha colored skin. He had spiked hair, which was something unusual among professors. He was very humble, approachable and always ready to help the students. He believed in caring about the students who showed real interest in the course and he did not show any interest in the inattentive students in the classroom. As usual, Vishu along with his friends was sitting on the last bench and they were busy in their own world. Avi and Vishu were playing a car-racing game on their cell phones. Sivu and Srini were discussing the latest movies in Bangalore. Except for the first two rows in the class the rest of the students, much like these four friends, were involved in issues outside of the classroom.

All of a sudden, Vishu's attention was diverted from the car game on his cell phone to the ongoing topic on engines and how they work. He was always fascinated about vehicles and wanted to know more about the functioning of engines. Professor Ashish Choudary explained the intricacies of an engine. He mentioned the different strokes or stages during the working of an engine. He summarized that there were

Inlet, Compression, Expansion and Exhaust strokes in case of a four-stroke engine. By now, Vishu was all ears as the Professor went on to describe various kinds of engines, namely petrol vs. diesel engine, four-stroke vs. two-stroke engine etc. It set Vishu thinking when Professor ended the topic about engines mentioning that it was a pity that other alternatives for these fuel engines, which were less harmful to nature, were not widely used. Once the class was over, all four headed to the cafeteria in the campus. As the three went and placed the order, Vishu agreed to find a table for them. He found an empty table and dumped his bag on it. He sat on the chair and started wondering about the design of the engine. He soon got lost in his thoughts. His reverie was disturbed once his friends got their food to the table. As the laughter continued, Vishu saw that his friends had made him dip his fingers in the hot coffee, which they had ordered. He then told them about the dream and how he had demonstrated a water engine at the Big Bang Day event.

They finished their coffee and started to walk out from the cafeteria. Avi asked, "How is this even possible? How can you make an engine work on just water?"

Vishu replied, "Why is this not possible? I explained the design I saw in my dream, didn't I?"

""Kannidhu kurdanadangge" which literally means - you are blind even with your eyes. There is a glaring flaw in the design. It is quite obvious that you cannot generate the enormous amount of energy required for an engine to function with just water movement. There are bursts of huge amounts of energy released every time the fuel enters the piston chamber causing the piston move back and forth. The same cannot be simulated with just the flow of water," explained Sivu. As Vishu listened to Sivu, he pondered on the whole idea of using water. They continued walking towards the Katte when Srini spoke for the first time after hearing Vishu's dream. "Come up with something that seems practical Vishu. Dreams are just dreams. What works in reality are the ideas that can be implemented."

Vishu was little irked and he blurted, "I do not know how to see dreams that are realistic and practical. As long as they keep me happy, I am fine with them." They reached the Katte and settled down on the bench below the tree. As they did not have any interesting topic to talk about, they sipped their coffee and were watching students pass by.

Vishu suddenly cried out aloud, "Sivu, look there's your girl heading out."

Sivu asked, "Where?"

"To your left!"

"I will be right back then," and Sivu walked towards her.

"Hey! Curly! Stop. Wait for me," yelled Sivu to a girl walking out of the parking lot. He walked towards her and gave a hi-five to her.

"Don't call me by that name," she whined. "I prefer being addressed as Sahana within college."

Sahana Rao was a girl from the Computer Science department as well. She was a tall, lean girl with curly hair. She wore rectangular framed spectacles, which gave her a geeky look. She spent most of her time reading. She was brought up in Bangalore but was born in a neighboring town. After coming to DCE, her life mostly revolved around the department and the library until she met Sivu. He had tried very hard to change her habit and was successful to a certain extent. Sivu had met her in the department for the first time and they both gotten along very well since then. They used to hang out after class every day. She stayed in the girls' dorm within campus and Sivu stayed behind longer in campus before leaving for his own dorm. They spent time walking around campus, talking in the café for hours, occasionally going out to catch a movie or for an early dinner. Since DCE had strict timing restrictions for the students in the dorm, they had to be back in college before dark.

"Movie today? Evening show followed by dinner?" asked Sivu.

"Which one? I need to get back soon, I have a lot of assignments pending."

"Don't worry. I will get my scooter and we can get back early."

"Yeah right! You have been talking about your scooter for ages. Every single time there is some mechanical problem and end up leaving it behind. Why do you have that piece of junk with you in the first place?"

"This time you will get to see it. Or we could go in your scooter as usual," smiled Sivu.

"You got new glasses? It looks different from the previous one."

"Well, these are the new prescription glasses. I went for an eye exam and my near-sightedness seems to have worsened. So, I need to wear these glasses all the time. Check out the new frame I got." He removed his spectacles and handed it to her.

She took a look at it and asked, "A red-framed one? Of all the colors, you got this?"

"What's wrong with red? I don't get it. Even my friends asked me the same question yesterday."

"Nothing wrong! You had so many colors to pick from and you pick a bold color. That amuses me."

"You need to keep up with the changing trends. Bold colors are the new flavor of the season. You will soon learn and I will help you out," teased Sivu.

"Whatever!" They stood there and spoke for few more minutes. All the while, Vishu and the others were looking at both of them from Katte.

Vishu stood up and bellowed, "Sivu! Sivu!" He turned around to other two and excitedly said, "Come on guys. Join me in pulling his leg. It's his turn to get ragged." The other two showed no interest in distracting Sivu. Vishu got irked at the lack of support.

"Now, why won't you support me?" Vishu growled. "You guys always pull my leg when I am talking to Akhila."

"It is funny to see you when we tease you. Sivu's is a different situation. He will not get distracted and it's no fun ragging him," joked Srini.

"Losers. I will get my chance someday to return the favor. Just wait!" Sivu returned to their gang on the Katte in a while and Sahana headed towards the department.

"I wish I could talk like you. I find it difficult to express my thoughts to a girl," grumbled Vishu.

"It is simple. How you converse with us is the same way you converse with the fairer sex," replied Sivu.

"You need to learn a unique way of talking,

Listening to which, she should start smiling;

Embark on the journey where your effort is put to test,

My friend, I wish you all the very best!" recited Avi.

"What is stopping you from doing that?" asked Sivu.

"I always run out of topics to talk about and end up wrapping the conversation soon."

"Hmm… You might be better off making a list of topics beforehand if it helps," suggested Avi.

"Good idea. I need to try that out on some girl."

"Why some girl? You know someone who likes you. What more do you need?" replied Srini.

"Not sure about her. I need some more time before I could ask her out," sighed Vishu.

Sivu took out a course book from his bag and said in Kannada, " 'Halliddaga kadle illa, kadle idhaga hallilla' which literally translates to 'those who have teeth don't have nuts and those who have nuts don't have teeth'. You have a girl who likes you and you don't like her; others want a girl and they don't have one. Anyways, take your time. The other two can find someone they like next week. Till then, focus on the tests starting tomorrow."

Srini curiously asked, "What do we have next week?"

Avi excitedly replied, "Next week is the biggest fest amongst all engineering colleges in Karnataka. Students from other colleges will visit the fest. It is the first time we will be experiencing it since we joined college. It's UTSAV dude!"

Chapter 4

The tests at DCE were conducted thrice before the final exams at the end of a semester. This was an opportunity for students to score one fourth of the semester's grade without a lot of blood, sweat and tears. As the exams were usually tough to crack and score good grades, the professors were lenient while grading the tests. Only a few studious students in each department sincerely prepared for the tests while the rest had their own means of filling up the answer sheets during the tests. Every student had a unique skill at gaining a good grade, the common running theme amidst all the students, however was to get as many marks as possible. They knew that this was their only chance as the final exams were conducted in a stricter environment at DCE and getting caught at that time would result in failing the exam. Srini was walking briskly, with a book that had a blue cover in his hand, and Vishu was trying to catch up to him. Both were in a hurry to reach the classroom early on the day of the third test of the semester.

Srini asked casually, pointing to the book in his hand, "Do you know why this is called a blue book?"

"I have no clue. You should be asking Sivu. I am sure he will have a ready answer in Kannada," replied Vishu, panting heavily and trying to match Srini's fast gait.

The blue book was the one in which the students were supposed to write their tests. Many had no clue as to why the book was named that way and Vishu was one of them. They reached their classroom to find out that they were one of the first few to have come and that was what they exactly wanted. Both of them did not have the skills to copy from chits or handmade notes that students illegally carried into tests. So, they came up with their own way of dealing with the situation. They used to write, in an abbreviated manner, details of potential topics that might be asked in the tests on the desks. Since nobody paid too much attention to what was written on the desks, these two did not have to worry about getting caught. And even if they were caught, they would simply claim that the writing was present beforehand on the desks and that they did not write anything.

Both selected the last but one desk and started filling in the content on the desk. The students gradually began pouring into the classroom. Avi came and sat in the desk ahead of the one that was selected by Vishu and Srini. Avi did not worry about the tests because he was generally well prepared ahead of time. Plus, he had the skill set to make small chits and refer to them when needed during the tests. After a couple of minutes, Sivu entered the classroom wearing his usual six pockets trousers and sat next to Avi. The purpose of six pockets trousers was to keep micro photocopies of important sections of the chapters in different pockets. The micro photocopies would be smaller than the average palm and easily fit inside the trousers' pockets.

Srini called out to Sivu and asked, "Why do you think they call this the 'Blue Book'?" pointing at the book on the desk. Sivu thought for a minute before replying. "It is like one of those idioms, 'Until blue in the face'. We try to explain the concepts that we have studied for the tests until we are blue in the face but the Professors do not understand

and give us low grades in the tests. I think some exasperated student came up with the name to mock the whole system."

"Wow. That is good reasoning dude. We believed your expertise was only in Kannada when it came to idioms. I am impressed!" Srini quipped. Before Srini could continue any further, everyone in the classroom was startled by the commotion in the corridor outside. After a few seconds, a group of Professors came inside and one of them announced, "Students, please take your belongings and go to the adjacent classroom, the test will be held there. It will be starting in the next five minutes."

A murmur started among the students and they began vacating the classroom. The faces of Vishu and Srini were a sight to behold. They were perplexed as they had not prepared for the test and their foolproof idea of referring to the content they wrote on the desk seemed next to impossible now. Both stood in silence, wondering what to do.

Vishu came up with an idea. He excitedly said, "Let's carry the desk to the other classroom." Srini looked a little confused.

"Are you nuts?" questioned Srini.

"Do you have any other bright idea? If not, then we are left with no option, aren't we?"

"But what if we get caught?"

"We will not be allowed to write the test. Given the current scenario, without the desk it is as good as not writing the test. Right?"

"Hmm. yeah. That's right."

Srini agreed reluctantly.

"Then let's get to work right away. Lift the other end of the desk."

They took the desk outside the classroom to the adjacent room where the test was supposed to be held leaving their classmates baffled. A couple of people asked why the desk had to be moved. Srini and Vishu proceeded without replying to those questions only to be stopped by the Professor, who had made the announcement in the previous classroom, at the entrance of the room. The Professor questioned, "Why are you dragging this desk here? Put that down!"

They placed the desk on the floor. Vishu replied, "This desk belongs to this classroom and somebody moved it out yesterday. We are just putting it back."

"Who moved it out in the first place and why?" questioned the Professor.

Vishu fumbled with words. "SSS-Sir, I... I... am not aware of who moved it out of here and why. Ah... Err... We were just standing outside the classroom yesterday when it was taken from here."

The Professor stood there not saying anything for a while. Srini did not dare open his mouth. Vishu had become a nervous wreck by then. He wasn't good at handling such sticky situations. Many a time, he would talk out of nervousness when caught doing things like this. This time was no different. He had too many things in mind. He was expecting the Professor to count the number of desks in the classroom; how easy it would have been for him to just skip the test; what the punishment they might have to undergo now would be. He tried to block all his thoughts, but in vain. The Professor broke the silence and yelled at Vishu to move the desk inside quickly. Relieved that they were not caught, they took the desk and placed it in the last row of the other classroom. Sivu and Avi followed them and settled in the second to last desk. A Professor who taught a course in the current semester distributed the question papers. Few minutes into the test, everyone in the classroom was busy filling the blue book either honestly with what they had studied the previous day or with their cheating skills. The rest of the test was surprisingly uneventful. The tests at DCE usually spread out over three consecutive days with two tests on each day. At the end of the third day of the test, everyone was relieved and left the classroom block in an excited daze. Once outside the block, these four guys saw a group of students staring at the wall. A closer look by Sivu confirmed that these students were actually reading the posters displayed on the wall.

Sivu cried out, "It's Utsav! Posters everywhere talking about the events."

The other three were reading them out loud. Avi read, "Utsav is incomplete without 'U' and 'V'!"

Vishu exclaimed, "Bulls are back!" The intercollegiate fest Utsav conducted at DCE had a Bull as the mascot. The students were engrossed in the list of events of the fest and they picked the events that they wanted to participate in or go as the audience.

Vishu asked, "How about attending the gaming event Srini?"

Srini reciprocated by nodding his head. "I am participating in the treasure hunt. Anyone cares to join me?" asked Sivu.

"I need to be present at the music competition that is at the same time as treasure hunt. You need to find a different partner for that. Later, I am going to participate in dumb charades," explained Avi.

Srini finished reading the poster and said, "Whichever competition you both attend, make it a point to meet us at the Katte before 4:30 PM tomorrow. We cannot afford to miss Mad Ads, which starts at 5:00 PM and the fashion show following that. If you guys are interested then we can meet a little earlier for the rock show too."

Both Sivu and Avi understood that it was more of an order than a request from Srini and they quietly agreed. On most occasions Srini called the shots and the rest invariably agreed; this was one such occasion. All four settled down on the Katte to spend time talking about the fest and attending different events. They finalized the time at which they would gather at the campus and headed towards their respective rooms after calling it a day.

It was still early next morning when Srini woke up with a severe headache. He got up and stared at the window in front of his bed for some time. For no good reason, he slapped his face twice. Staring at his shadow on the wall he wondered why he had just slapped himself. On his way to the bathroom, he kicked an empty water bottle lying on the ground. He became perplexed, as he did not kick it intentionally. Irked by the way the morning was unfolding, he continued further to the bathroom.

He picked up his toothpaste and toothbrush. Just as he was about to apply the paste on the brush, he squeezed the toothpaste so hard that he ended up emptying the entire tube on the brush. Having wasted a full tube of toothpaste at one go, he started thinking about what was going wrong and the reasons behind his actions as even this recent one was again not under his control. Horror movies he had watched flashed across his mind and he immediately rejected it, reminding himself that the movies were nothing more than fiction. He cursed his fate and proceeded to wash off the excess paste on the brush by opening the tap. Involuntarily his hand went to the hot water tap and turned it on full. He screamed out of pain and moved his hands away from the stream of scalding water. As he pulled his hand out of the way he saw a shadow dart across the wall behind him in the mirror.

He stood there in complete silence watching his shadow on the wall. For a minute, everything seemed normal. Breathing heavily and sweating profusely, he continued to stare at his shadow. Sweat started to trickle down his forehead. He waited patiently, like a hunter waiting for prey, without moving an inch. To his horror, he saw that his shadow proceeded to turn on the shower and he was made to do the same within a fraction of a second. As he witnessed this fear enveloped him and his heart skipped a beat. It was his shadow that was making him do all these things since morning. Petrified by the unusual happenings, he left the bathroom in a hurry.

Keeping a close watch on his shadow, Srini quickly changed his clothes and got ready to leave for college. He picked up the perfume bottle to spray it on to his clothes and ended up spraying it on to his face. He cried out in pain and realized that it was because of his shadow. He saw that the shadow placed its hands on the hips and moved the body as if it resembled a person laughing out loudly. Soon, he was forced to imitate and started laughing with his hands placed on his hips. He got very angry because instead of wiping perfume off his face, he was made to laugh at his own plight. Hurriedly, he wiped his face and left the room. He started walking towards college, staring at his shadow every now and then. He came to a traffic signal and had to wait to cross the road. He saw a few eunuchs doing their usual rounds of collecting money from the motorists. Quickly, he turned towards his shadow anticipating another episode. His guess turned out to be right as he saw his shadow moving his right hand towards his face. Anxiously, he waited to be forced to follow the same. He realized the hand went to his mouth and he whistled at the eunuchs near the traffic signal. Before he could prevent further damage, his hand went up in the air and waved to them exactly imitating his shadow's actions.

The eunuchs got excited and ran towards Srini. They started singing and dancing around him. People around eyed him curiously embarrassing him. He tried in vain to leave the place. He ended up paying some money to the eunuchs and wriggled out of that place and walked away with his head down. Srini continued walking briskly without stopping anywhere till he reached the college campus. He entered the college feeling a little relieved that the rest of the journey to the campus was uneventful. He checked his watch and it was almost time for his class to begin and headed towards his classroom block. He hoped that the worst was behind him.

On the way, he saw a bunch of girls standing and chatting. Without raising his head, he continued to walk, as he had no intentions of getting into trouble again. But his shadow had different plans for him. He came to a standstill a few feet away from the group. He nervously looked at his shadow for the next move. He started waving his hand at the girls and one of the girls in the group noticed him and turned. He saw his shadow take his hand to his face and move it forward. Before he could realize what he was going to do, his hand reached his mouth and went forward. He realized that he just gave a flying kiss to an unknown girl on campus. His face turned red and stood rooted to the spot. The girl got offended and approached him furiously. She slapped Srini and swore at him for his misbehavior. Her group of friends supported her and they all swore at him for his actions. Unable to explain his situation, he apologized for his behavior to the girl and dejectedly turned back to walk out of campus.

Reminiscing about how things had unfolded during the day, Srini left the campus, dejected and upset. He walked at a slow pace on the footpath next to the college compound. He reached an intersection and waited for his turn to cross the road. Meanwhile, a truck speeding on the lane right next to the footpath approached the intersection where Srini was waiting. Aware of the distant truck, he patiently waited for it to pass before crossing the road. Momentarily, he turned to checkout his shadow's antics. He was shocked to see that the shadow prepared itself to jump on to the lane where the truck was speeding towards him. Before he had any time to react, he too had jumped! The truck made a screeching sound as the driver stomped on the brakes. Srini closed his eyes and screamed out of sheer terror.

"He screams at the top of his voice and falls off the bed. He wakes up sweating profusely and realizes that this was all one horrible nightmare. Sharp rays of sunlight glean through the drapes of his bedroom window. He stands by the window carefully getting his shadow to cast on the wall in front. The shadow made the poster on the wall look dull. But it did not move. Things were normal again. Srini heaves a sigh of relief and the camera focuses slowly on the shadow. This is where we stop and show the credits," said Vishu to his friends at the Katte.

The four of them had met at the campus on the morning of the fest. As planned, Vishu and Srini went to participate in the gaming competition. They were eliminated in the very first round. Both spent some time watching others play and then they visited other competitions. Sivu participated in the treasure hunt partnering with one of the friends, Divya, from the information science department. They were able to reach the final clue but could not figure out what it was within the stipulated time. Meanwhile, Avi had completed his music competition and was participating in dumb charades with two other teammates from his department. Srini, Sivu and Vishu were among the audience for that event. Avi went along with the other three to watch the short film competition. Once they were done with it, they walked to the Katte. Vishu started explaining his idea for a short film and portrayed Srini as the protagonist. He walked them through scene by scene about how Srini would be tormented by his own shadow. Once he was done telling the story, Vishu was eager to know his friends' feedback. Vishu asked the others, "What do you think about this story as an outline for a short film? I am really interested in directing one."

"The idea is excellent. With a little effort, you should be able to pull it off," complimented Sivu.

Vishu nodded and looked at others for their views. Srini was excited. He said, "It is good for a first draft. I feel the story needs to be improvised, at least the way it ends."

"I second that. I enjoyed the story till the end. Maybe what Srini is suggesting is that you can improvise the way it ends. When the camera focuses on the shadow, make the shadow to dance or better disappear and then show the credits. This way, you are ending your story with a punch," said Avi.

Vishu listened to them quietly without saying anything. He was assimilating the details given by his friends. Srini, seeing Vishu's reactions, patted him on the back and said,

"I would be more than glad to be the protagonist. We could aim at participating in the next short film competition. "

"You thought it would be like baking a cake,

But soon from your dreams, you did wake;

Lots of time, we have to make,

And that would be nothing, for your sake!" quoted Avi in his style.

Vishu smiled and replied, "Thanks for your support guys."

Srini glanced at his watch and it was time for the rock show at the Sir M Visvesvaraya stadium. He alerted the other guys and they all headed towards the stadium. The crowd had already gathered and the first couple of rows were occupied. The four guys managed to find a spot in the middle and they settled down. The show started with the local DJ wooing the crowd with some of the latest hits. Most engineering colleges in Bangalore participated in the event with their rock bands. The energy of the crowd amplified whenever the slogan "Bulls are Back" was chanted in a catchy and rhythmic tune. The event stretched over a couple of hours and by then, Srini had already lost his patience sitting, as this event was not his cup of tea. Even his friends who had convinced him to come in the first place could not keep him there any longer.

'Mad Ads' was the next event and it started within a few minutes following the end of the rock show. Students had hardly any time to grab something to eat from the refreshment counters before the event began. 'Mad Ads' was one of those shows that required synchrony, as there would be one narrator speaking for all the actors. This was more of a monologue combined with an actor group. They had to maintain the flow without which the story would not look funny. It required talent and practice to pull off something like this in a big event like the UTSAV. Teams from other colleges started performing and the crowd cheered every performance with applause. By then, it had become dark and the lights were turned on and the stage had spotlights of different colors hovering around it. It was finally time for the much-awaited show of the fest, the 'Fashion show' and UTSAV was also known for this event. It was an opportunity for the students to see and comment about the fairer sex wearing skimpy clothes and walking on the ramp. The models began walking the ramp with elegance and poise. Finally, DCE's very own team from the Architecture branch stole the show. The Architecture department was quite well-known for good-looking girls and they took the fashion show event to the next level. The UTSAV fest ended with the audience shouting "Bulls are back" slogan and bursting of crackers by the organizers. Once the festivities died down, all their classmates met up near the Katte to catch up before calling it a day. And what a fantastic day it had turned out to be for them! The memories of the fest were etched in their minds forever.

CHAPTER 5

A week after the fest, the four guys had finished their classes for the day and were taking a break at their usual place, the Katte. It was getting darker and very few students lingered as most of them had left for the day. The lights around the campus were not turned on yet. A half-moon was already peeking at a distance from the east. The cool breeze lent itself to a soothing atmosphere and the guys were not ready to leave the campus just yet. They just wanted to sit there and kill time enjoying the weather. Nitesh, their classmate was walking towards them and it seemed like he was in a hurry. He neared the Katte and shot a question at Vishu.

"Oh hey, Vishu! Care to join us at Haze today? A bunch of us are planning to go there tonight."

Haze was the only pub close to the DCE campus and many students spent a lot of time after college hours there. Most pubs asked for an ID to check the age of the visitors in order to ensure that liquor was not served to underage students. Haze, however chose to overlook that requirement. It also offered discounts on big parties of students, thereby attracting a whole lot of them. "I am going to pass on Haze. I don't like any liquid that controls my mind," Vishu continued, "You go ahead. But…"

"Catch you later then! Bye." Vishu was planning to ask if it was okay for the other three to join him but he was interrupted. Before he could say anything, Nitesh left the place. Vishu got really angry at his behavior and started cursing him. "Asshole! Why didn't he even wait to listen? I was going to ask if you guys could join him."

"It is fine bro! Relax," replied Srini.

"How is it fine? We all belong to the same department and he invited me alone. He pretended as if you people are not here at all."

"Calm down. Anyways, we would not have accompanied his group," said Sivu.

"Why not? And why did he not invite you three? What have you guys been up to?" yelled Vishu.

"Nothing. We have not done anything to annoy him for sure."

Vishu reluctantly agreed to that and said, "Then what was that guy's problem?"

"You need to take this easy. It's not a big deal. No point haggling about the same topic," pacified Srini.

"Why didn't you go along with him? And what is that dialogue about liquid and controlling your mind?" asked Avi.

"That was just to ward him off. I have something already planned for tonight."

"What's cooking here?"

"Nothing. Just the usual."

"Out with it. Where are you planning to go?" questioned Sivu.

"Well, I have asked Akhila out for a date. I am planning to take her out to dinner."

"Your face goes red coz you blush,

Take her tonight to some place plush;

We reckon she is quite beautiful,

May your lives be wonderful!" quoted Avi enthusiastically.

"Thanks Avi. I hope so."

"Wow! That is amazing. How come someone finally decided?" asked Srini curiously.

"I had been thinking for the past few days about her and yesterday I decided to propose to her."

"Brilliant! Atta boy! I have full faith in you. Go get your girl," cheered Sivu.

"Thanks Sivu. Hopefully things will go well."

"Where are you taking her tonight? What is the plan?" queried Avi.

"Suspense! Tomorrow I will tell you guys. Till then, you all need to wait."

After a while, Vishu left to his room to freshen up before the big date. They had decided that he would be picking Akhila at seven in the evening from college. He had booked a table for two in a roof top restaurant on Mahatma Gandhi Road also known as M G Road. Vishu reached college by 7:00 PM and saw that Akhila was already waiting for him at the rendezvous point. She wore a sleeveless maroon dress with a frill trim at the knee. She had straightened her hair and let it cascade down her back. Vishu also spotted brownish streaks in her tresses, which complemented the color of the dress she wore. Her heels added a few more inches to her height. She was not wearing a lot of jewelry apart from simple earrings and a bracelet. The intoxicating fragrance of her perfume completed her look, a very attractive look thought Vishu.

Vishu had bought a bouquet on his way to the college. "You are looking beautiful. Some flowers for the lady," he said while handing them over to Akhila.

"Thank you. You are looking good too!" Akhila accepted the bouquet blushingly.

Vishu's attire was simple yet befitting a party. He wore a full-sleeved black shirt with blue denim jeans and brown leather shoes. He had applied a leave-in conditioner, which he rarely did, and combed his hair back. He was clean-shaven because of which he looked much younger than he would look usually. They took a taxi to reach M G Road, as that was the fastest way to commute. The idea was to spend more time at the restaurant. It took them just over forty minutes to reach the place. Since they arrived a few minutes prior to their reservation, they stood outside talking. The talk was causal and most importantly, both of them were enjoying each other's company.

All the while, the proposal loomed large in Vishu's mind and he was unable to focus. What should he say to her and how? Do it before dinner or soon after it? Or does he wait till they are outside on the road? He could not stop himself from thinking about the proposal whatsoever. They took the elevator to the 13th floor for the restaurant. On special request from Vishu, they were given the table next to the railings with a view of the metro station and the cricket stadium. The UB city skyline and Cubbon Park were to the left of the stadium. The tables were spaced apart to allow for privacy, just the way Vishu wanted, and it was not very crowded at that moment. He started to contemplate the proposal in the beginning once the wine was served. He thought he would raise a toast to the lovely lady and then propose.

They placed their orders and continued talking about their childhood and their families. The wine was served along with the appetizers. Vishu tried to muster up the courage to raise a toast to the lady but he was unable to find the right timing. Akhila kept talking, without allowing enough room for Vishu to say anything. He listened to her patiently wondering if he would ever get a chance to propose to her. The entrees were ordered and served rather quickly. She was now reminiscing about her fond memories on M G Road as she was brought up in Bangalore. How often her parents took her to M G Road; the walks along the boulevard that she had enjoyed as a kid; hot corn or groundnuts that her dad bought for her; colorful balloons that she carried back home. She went on and on. There was no stopping her. Time flew by without Vishu's realization. They were almost done with their dinner. Vishu had half a mind to interrupt her and tell her that he had something more important to talk about. He avoided cutting her off while she was speaking, thinking he would come across as being rude. He nodded all the while waiting for the right moment that never came. Vishu paid the bill and they both stepped out of the restaurant. Since they had finished their dinner early, Vishu suggested that they go for a walk on the ramp beside the metro. Besides that he still was waiting for the opportunity to propose. They took the stairs in front of the metro station and got on to the walkers' ramp. The ramp was sparsely populated at that moment. It was well lit and security guards were present at the entrance of the ramp. Despite the odd hours, people felt secure enough to go for a walk and enjoy the weather along with the view.

Vishu and Akhila walked slowly discussing their interests and hobbies. They continued for a couple of minutes before coming to a standstill at one of the viewpoints facing the stadium. Traffic had reduced to a great extent and it was peaceful at that spot. Both inched towards the railings and they stood looking at the sky. The sky was clear with a sheer blanket of twinkling stars. The half-moon was at his best with full vigor and brightness. She spoke after a couple of minutes of silence.

"I am enjoying it. I love this moment." She stood there watching the stadium lights and relishing the moment. He was standing beside her. He knew this was the time and jumped on it. He moved slowly and stood behind her. He quietly stretched his both hands and held the railings, encircling her. Slowly, he came forward and leaned a little towards her ears. He was so close to her that she could hear him breathe but she stood rooted without reacting. He spoke gently without any hesitation.

"I love this weather; I love this view; I love this moment and above all, I love you!"

He continued as she listened. "I want this time to freeze forever. I want you by my side. I would love to walk with you, step for a step throughout my life. Will you become part of my life? Do you feel the same way about me?"

She quietly turned around and faced him. From her face, it looked as if she had predicted this moment would occur. Nevertheless, she was mum and did not say a word. Her face was glowing in the moonlight. She was shy and did not look at his face. He held her shoulders and then tenderly lifted her face with his fore finger. She was blushing profusely and her cheeks had turned red. She continued to look down. He spoke softly and patiently.

"Look at me. I want to know what you think. Your silence is not helping me. I promise to take care of you for the rest of my life. I will look after your…"

"Sir, here's your check," said a gruff voice from behind.

Vishu was startled to hear a male voice. He turned around to realize that he was still at the restaurant and it was the waiter who had got the check. He looked in the front to see Akhila was getting back to the table from the restroom. It struck him that he had asked for the check and meanwhile she had left the table for a few minutes. He felt miserable in the real world after the glorious moment in his dreams. He paid the amount to the waiter and they both waited for the change. Suddenly from behind, he could hear someone calling his name.

"Hey Vishu!" It was Sanjana, his classmate from pre-university. "How are you doing? Long time since we caught up." She was a sweet girl and Vishu used to hang out with her while in college. He, for some reason, always thought she had a crush on him. He was little taken aback to see her over there at that moment.

"Sanjana! I am fine. Yep, the last we met was before college started. How have you been?"

"Never better!" She noticed another girl at the table and looking at her she asked Vishu, "I hope I am not interrupting."

"Not at all. This is Akhila, my college mate. Akhila, meet Sanjana, my pre-university friend."

After the formal pleasantries and handshakes, "I got to go now. It was nice meeting you, Akhila. And Vishu, do plan something soon and let's catch up sometime," she said winking at Vishu and before leaving she said, "You guys have fun. Take care."

"You too. Bye!"

"Who is she?" asked Akhila once Sanjana stepped out of the restaurant.

"I told you. She is a friend from my pre-university days."

"And?"

"And what? I used to hang around with her but nothing serious though. She's a smart girl, used to help me with the assignments all the time."

"Oh I see. Good," said Akhila nonchalantly. They got the change from the waiter and Vishu tipped him generously. Once they came out of the restaurant, they thought of walking for some distance before taking the cab back to college. The roads were deserted and only a few motorists were zipping past them. Most shops were closed and very few people were on the street.

"By the way, why did she wink at you before leaving?"

Vishu rolled his eyes. He could not believe that Akhila was jealous of some girl who spoke to him. He liked the fact that he could evoke such emotions in her.

"Ah… I am not sure. I guess it is her way of wishing her friends." Akhila did not buy it. She walked without saying anything. By the look on her face, it was clear that she was mad at Vishu.

"Listen. She was a good friend and I liked hanging out with her. I have many friends like her who are close to me. They all are good friends and that's it. Alright?"

"I understand now. I am just another girl in your life!" Vishu took a minute to process it. It hit him badly and he was not sure how to tackle her words. He had come tonight with the intention of proposing to her and this was something he had not expected.

"No! No! Ahh… You are not. I was mentioning that these were just friends and…"

"Vishu, it is fine! I got the point loud and clear. I am just another girl in your life. That's it!"

He froze as he did not to know what to do. Things were falling apart and he felt the intense fear of losing her forever. He held her shoulders and made her stop. She was not ready to see his face as she was angry and she kept looking down.

"Hold on for a minute and look at me. I have something to tell you." She was trying to free herself from him and wanted to walk away from there.

"Leave me Vishu. Let me go." Vishu raised his tone and said, "Listen to what I have to say. You are free to go after that." She faced him with folded hands and was ready to hear him out.

"See… How do I put it? Hmm… Let me try." He cleared his voice and in a soft tone he said by looking into her eyes, "You are not just another girl in my life. You are the one with whom I want to spend my rest of the life. You are the girl of my life! I love you Akhila. Do you love me?" Finally the moment had come and he looked at her eagerly for her response. She was very happy and she could not hide her smile from him. She had been waiting to hear these words for a long time.

"Yes. I do," replied Akhila coyly. Vishu was ecstatic to hear a positive response from her. He stepped ahead and hugged her for a few minutes. He held her close to his chest and stood there with his arms around her. They spent some time together on M G Road before heading back to college. Vishu dropped her to the hostel and started towards his room. He wanted to share the happy news with his friends but it was already very late so he had to wait till the next morning. The following day, Vishu met the rest of his friends at Katte and excitedly shared his experience with them. All three congratulated him and patted his back. They were really happy to hear the good news. Vishu described each and every event from the previous day and they were all ears. He also explained to them about his dream and how he had already proposed to her in the dream. Then how things went bad and finally how he ended up actually proposing to the girl he loved.

"Awesome. I told you yesterday that I had full faith in you. At last, it ended on a good note and only that matters," praised Sivu.

"Thanks Sivu."

"Have you met her today? When are you meeting her?" asked Sivu.

"Not yet. I will be meeting her soon."

"Go meet her now."

"I will leave in sometime. She will come to the cafeteria."

"Good for you. I am heading over to meet Sahana in the library. Catch you guys later." Sivu bid goodbye and headed towards the library. Srini and Avi continued to talk to Vishu for some more time. It was all about his adventures of last night and how he saved the day in the end. Later, Vishu too left to the cafeteria to meet Akhila. Meanwhile in the library café lounge, Sivu met Sahana who was listening to songs on her laptop. He abruptly closed the laptop and told her how his close friend Vishu had proposed Akhila. She was overjoyed to hear.

"Very nice. So everything went well?"

"Yes, eventually!" exclaimed Sivu.

"Cool. Where were you yesterday?"

"I was just hanging out with friends. You need to hear about Vishu's messing up in the beginning and how he finally managed everything in the end."

"Go on. Tell me."

As they started walking towards the silent area in the library, Sivu told her about the events that occurred the previous night between Vishu and Akhila. Once they entered the silent area, Sivu continued to whisper and they picked an isolated spot next to a window. Sahana unpacked her bag and removed the laptop as she listened to Sivu. She placed the laptop on the table and plugged the charger to the socket nearby. Once she flipped opened the laptop, it started playing music loudly. The volume control keys had become inactive and Sahana was unable to neither stop the music nor reduce the volume. By now, everyone in the silent room was staring at them and they both got nervous. She picked up the laptop and ran out from the silent room. Onlookers burst out laughing at her plight. The librarian, Mr. Pradeep Shankar, stopped her near the café just outside the silent room. Before she could explain anything to him, Sivu reached over there after grabbing all her belongings from the silent room. The music was still playing loudly and her efforts to stop it were futile.

"What is all this nuisance? Do you even realize that this is a library and not a disco?" shouted the librarian.

"I am sorry Sir. I can't seem to get it to stop. I need to leave!" Sahana apologized and left the place carrying the laptop with her. She did not wait for the librarian's reply. He was livid seeing her walk out.

"Wait. Stop right there," the Librarian cried out.

"I am so sorry, Sir. It was an accident and we are not able to stop the music," apologized Sivu.

"Do you have any common sense at all? There are certain protocols every student must follow here."

The librarian continued to yell at Sivu for some more time before letting him go. He walked out of the library and saw that Sahana had stopped the music somehow. Once he gave Sahana her belongings, she started scolding him.

"It is all your fault. I felt so embarrassed over there. Everyone was laughing at us."

"What did I do?" asked Sivu. He was surprised to see that he was blamed without any reason.

"You were the one who closed the laptop when it was still playing music. It continued to play soon after it was opened again." Tears rolled out from her eyes but she was still mad at him.

"I am sorry. Now, will you stop crying? Nothing has happened."

"Leave me alone. I will talk to you later."

"Listen, Sahu. Cool down ..."

"Just leave. Now!" Dejected and helpless, Sivu left the place and walked slowly towards the Katte. He met the other three friends at the Katte after a while and narrated the entire library episode to them. Vishu had returned from the cafeteria by then. They tried to console him but he was in no mood to listen to anyone. "I am going to my room. I will meet you guys tomorrow."

"Do you remember that we have Computer Basics internal lab exam tomorrow morning?" asked Srini.

"Yes! I remember. I will prepare for that in the evening. Bye for now."

He left the place and other three continued to sit there and study before proceeding to their respective homes. The following day, all four met up near the computer science lab in the morning, an hour before the internal exam. The students had to attend one internal lab exam before the final lab exam every semester. The pattern of the exam was simple. They drew lots and picked a program to execute on the system. Following this was the viva, where they had to answer a few questions orally, related to the program they had just executed. In the end, the answer sheets containing the program and the output had to be submitted.

The exam started at 10:00 AM sharp. Batches of 15 students were randomly assigned to that slot beforehand. The internal examiner for the day was the lab instructor, Mrs. Jayashree Nath. She was quite strict with the way she handled things and students were usually very careful around her. They disliked her for being unfriendly and authoritative. She wore a serious face all the time and no one had seen her smile, ever. The entire batch was assigned programs within the first 10 minutes of the exam. Vishu went to the last row of computers in the lab and started writing the code on the answer sheet. The other three followed the same and sat beside him. Avi quickly finished writing and started typing them on the system. Sivu was the next to start typing the code. Srini and Vishu followed after a few more minutes. The lab instructor started conducting a viva even as the students were executing the program. She called each row of students and asked a couple of questions related to the program or course. By the time Vishu's row got called for the viva, all the four guys had finished executing the program. They had gotten easier programs, so they finished without any hassles. When the last row's turn came, all four went and sat in front of the lab instructor. She was busy entering marks to the previous batch of students and did not even look up. Vishu and others waited anxiously for her to ask the questions.

"Which is the best sorting algorithm according to you? And why?" she questioned without lifting her head.

"Sorting algorithm… Hmm… Bubble sort," answered Vishu. But he was not sure of the answer.

"Insertion sort would be my choice," replied Srini.

Both Srini and Vishu had ignored the viva completely as the marks allocated for it was less compared to executing the program. They thought of blabbering in the viva and getting done with it. But, Sivu had spent some time preparing for viva and he was not sure of the right answer. He felt this answer had multiple possibilities depending on the given set of conditions.

"Insertion sort is the best according to me," Sivu continued, "If I remember correctly, It has the best-case time efficiency compared to other algorithms."

Avi was silently listening to others' answers. He had prepared well for the viva and he knew the various different algorithms and their time efficiencies at the tip of his hands. "My choice would be Quick sort. Bubble sort clearly doesn't fall under the best algorithms for sorting because of its low efficiency. Insertion sort works well only in the best-case scenario and not in average and worst-case scenarios. Quick sort has good time efficiency for best-case and average-case scenarios. Worst-case scenario is equivalent to the sorting algorithms mentioned by others."

The lab instructor looked up for the first time and started staring at Vishu for giving the wrong answer. She didn't like him as he used to miss classes very often or be inattentive in class if he ever did attend. She looked particularly annoyed with him today as well.

"Once you are finished with the execution, put the answer sheet next to the system and leave. I will check the output later. We are finished here." She said it in an unpleasant tone and went back to entering marks for the previous batch of students. The other three were perplexed and didn't know what to do, whether to leave with Vishu or stay there for few more questions. Avi courageously ventured to ask her what they should do. He said, "Ma'am…"

Before he could proceed, she interrupted. Without even looking up she said, "You may go now! I am done." All four got up and left the lab instructor's table. They kept the answer sheet next to their systems, as told by her, and came out the lab. As they proceeded towards Katte, Srini opened his mouth.

"Avi, why did you do that?"

"What did I do?" Avi was confused.

"Negating others' answers. Why did you have to do that?"

"I just gave a detailed explanation," justified Avi.

"Agreed. But you could have done that without taking other examples of the algorithms," cried out Srini.

"Forget it. It is over now." interrupted Vishu. He continued, "Why blame him when we both did not prepare for viva in the first place?" Vishu was irked with himself as he had not spent any time preparing for the viva and he could not see someone taking the blame for his mistake.

"Alright! Let's change the topic. What plans for the day?" suggested Sivu.

"I am going now to meet Akhila. Will meet you all later if you guys are still around. Bye for now," said Vishu. He deviated from the admissions building and went towards the girls hostel.

"Bye!" The others went towards the Katte through the parking lot to spend some time before heading back to hostel.

CHAPTER 6

Couple of weeks went by and the weather in Bangalore got cooler by the day. Winter started to creep in and there was hardly any sign of sunshine. Akhila was wearing a black leather jacket, a white tee, blue jeans, stole around her neck, and black shoes to keep her warm. She met Vishu at the coffee kiosk and he got two hot coffees for them. He was dressed casually with black jeans and a green hoodie. They headed towards the stadium sipping their coffees. As the days had gone by, they both grew very close to each other and were spending more and more time together. Vishu enjoyed her company to a great extent and hardly met his other three friends.

Vishu suggested with a smirk, "Let me hold your hand."

"I am carrying a cup of coffee," Akhila replied curtly.

"I meant the other hand which is free."

"No! I am feeling cold and I do not want to take it out of the pocket."

Vishu felt a little sad, as he wanted to hold her hand and walk. Akhila noticed his reaction and got her hand out of the pocket, held his hand and snuggled it back into her pocket. "Problem solved. I have my hand inside my jacket pocket along with yours and you are holding my hand too." Vishu looked at her and smiled. He did not have words to express the happiness he found in small things like holding hands.

"Did you know that it has already been two weeks since I proposed to you? Time flies. Really!" exclaimed Vishu.

"I know. It feels like it was just last night."

"To be frank, I was very tensed that night. I must have spent the entire day thinking of a way to propose you."

"Oh yeah. Even after a day's thinking, you almost messed it up," laughed Akhila.

"Come on! What matters is that I did not. Also, who would have guessed that you would react the way you did? I guess it is true what they say, a woman's mind is very complicated."

"Yes! Any problems with that?" A smile played on her lips as she tried to pull Vishu's leg.

"None for now."

They entered the Sir M Visveswaraya stadium and Akhila suggested going around the track once before settling in the stands. They trashed the empty coffee cups in one of the dustbins nearby and they started walking on the track. "I have hardly met the guys in the last two weeks. They will be mad at me for sure."

"Srini, Sivu and Avi. Is that right?"

"Yep. My close friends from the first day of college," Vishu continued describing each one, "Srini is the cool guy and the boss in our group. Eventually, it is his decision that prevails. Sivu is the dude who has the knack to strike a conversation with anyone, especially with girls. He quotes idioms in Kannada at apt moments. Avi is a music lover and a studious guy. He has a penchant for reciting poetry on the fly."

"Oh that is cool."

"You must have seen them around on the first day when I was getting ragged."

"Nah, I don't remember. Once I meet them, I might recognize them. When will you introduce me to them?"

"Very soon. I have been trying to get hold of them. I mentioned this when we met but things are not falling in place."

"I guess they don't want to meet me," suggested Akhila.

"Why would that be? Nope, I don't think so. They will be glad to meet you."

"I am not sure. I just feel that way."

"Trust me. Everything is fine. I will introduce you to them soon. Actually, I am planning to meet them soon."

"Cool. You should spend more time with them."

"Yeah. Else I have to hear things from them," laughed Vishu, "And I will ask when they can meet you."

"Hmm. That works. Let me know." Akhila checked her watch and it was already quarter to noon. She remembered that she had an appointment with one of her professors at noon.

"Oh! I need to leave now," exclaimed Akhila.

"Why do you need to leave so early?"

"I totally forgot that I have an appointment with my Software Engineering professor in 15 minutes. I need to rush."

"Then what am I supposed to do?"

"You go and meet your friends. See if they are available now. Spend some time with them too."

"Alright. I will meet you in the evening at the Katte." They started walking out of the stadium. Akhila headed directly to her department building and Vishu went to Katte to meet his friends. They were sitting there talking.

"Hey! How is it going?"

"Guys, look who is here. Seeing you after a long time. How are you?" asked Srini. He stood up and hugged Vishu.

"I am good. I just met Akhila and thought I'll swing by," Vishu said, and went on rattling about Akhila and what they spoke; where they went; what they ate; etc. After a while, Avi could not take it any longer and he interrupted Vishu.

"Shall we go grab some coffee guys?"

"Cool. Let's go," said Vishu and realized that he had been the only one talking all this while and that too only about Akhila. They went to the nearby coffee kiosk and everyone got one except for Vishu. They returned to Katte and sat there sipping the hot coffee. Vishu asked, "How is it going for you Sivu? Last time we met, things were not okay between you and Sahana."

"Ah. Yeah. Everything is fine now. We patched up over a week ago or so. In fact, I met her today. We were goofing around with her laptop and clicked our photo using her webcam. I have asked her to email it to me."

"That's nice. Show it to us once you get it."

All of a sudden, there was a loud bark. Everybody turned around to look and they saw a stray dog that had come close to them. "Come here, Muffin. Come here! Good boy!" Avi began to pet the dog. Muffin was the name chosen by Avi. He used to pet him, hug him and play fetch with him. He had also taught him a few tricks.

"Ha. Why did you call him muffin? It is not a thing to eat. PETA guys might sue you for abusing a dog," joked Srini.

"I will name it whatever I want. PETA has nothing to do with the naming as long as I am not harming the dog. I enjoy playing with him and likewise he enjoys too," replied Avi.

"You keep squeezing the dog like that and it will die of suffocation one day. PETA will come behind you for sure that time," Sivu commented.

Avi pretended as if he did not hear the comment and continued playing with the dog. Srini turned to Vishu and asked, "What else? Any new dreams or ideas?"

"I was thinking of one the other day. I was not sure of the feasibility and did not want to tell you guys."

"Go on. You can share it with us," persisted Srini.

"Alright. Don't laugh after hearing it."

"Sure. We won't." assured Sivu.

"The other day I was looking at a calculator that I had with me. It is solar powered and has cells which get charged when exposed to sunlight. I am also aware of solar watches, which runs on a similar principle. There are streetlights that get their electric power from sun energy directly using the same solar cells."

By then Avi was all ears and he asked, "So what? One of your ideas is to generate electricity?"

"Exactly. I was thinking why shouldn't we extend it to powering buildings, offices, labs etc. I dreamt that a huge land covered with cells that can get charged during the daytime and power the buildings. I even saw fields or stadiums completely covered with those cells and producing loads of electricity."

"Those cells form a solar panel," clarified Sivu.

"Solar panel?"

"Yes. It is a package of photo-voltaic cells used to generate and supply electricity."

"Awesome. Then we use those solar panels and cover the entire land or field for generating electricity. We can also extend it to vehicles and use the solar panels as the vehicle's body instead. What do you guys think?" asked Vishu enthusiastically.

"Either you are living in a prehistoric world or your ideas are antiquated. I think it is the latter," replied Srini.

"What do you mean?"

"I am saying this because you are not aware of your surroundings. I feel this idea would have been excellent 10 years ago. Not today for sure," clarified Srini.

"How do you know? It might work well."

"I know because I have seen it. Come with me. I want you to see something."

"Where are we going now?" asked Vishu curiously.

"To the Sir M Visveswaraya stadium. Everybody, let's go."

"I just returned from the stadium. Do we really need to go there again? It seems like a kilometre away."

"Yes we do. Now come on. I am sure you will be thrilled," ordered Srini.

"What is there that I have not seen earlier?" quipped Vishu.

"Wait and see, my friend!"

Avi whispered something to muffin before walking along with others. The dog followed him to some distance before wandering off. Srini was pumped, eager to prove his point and he strode away in the direction of the stadium, the others were finding it difficult to match his speed. Avi and Sivu walked slowly whereas Vishu jogged next to Srini as he was curious to know what linked the stadium to his dream.

"Is it about electricity generation?" quipped Vishu. He could not resist asking questions to Srini any longer.

"You will get to know." Srini was in no mood to let the cat out of the bag so soon. He wanted to maintain the surprise till the end.

"Are we going to the center field in the stadium?"

"Nope. Not really."

Srini entered the archway and went straight towards the stands. The others followed him dutifully. He climbed the stairs and went to the top row in the stands. The view from the top was breathtaking. Vishu came and stood next to Srini and asked, "Now what?"

"All I ask is a little bit of patience." Srini continued walking to one end of the top row without waiting for the others to follow.

There was a grill gate at the end of the top row and Srini walked up to it. He noticed that gate was locked and sighed, "It's locked. Now, what do we do? Usually it is open and I have seen it."

"Where does this gate take you?" Sivu asked, curiously.

"To the terrace. I have been there and it is mind blowing. Breathtaking view of the stadium and the college," explained Srini. "I have seen a security guard around here and he may have the key. Let's try to find him."

Everybody heard a whistle blowing from the center field and they turned around to see the security guard coming towards them. Raju, the security guard at the stadium, was in his mid-forties. He was dark skinned, potbellied, five feet tall and sported a big moustache. His uniform was khaki colored and he used to carry a cane stick. He was an alcoholic and was suspended a couple of times for drinking during working hours.

"I will deal with him. You guys watch and learn," ordered Srini. Raju came to the top row and walked up to them swinging his stick in the air. The moment he came near them, they could smell the alcohol on his breath. Everyone took a step back in a hurry to put distance between them.

"What are you doing here? Students are not allowed here." His eyes were tinged red because of excessive drinking and he was finding it difficult to stand without swaying.

"Err... We just wanted to look around. We wanted to check out the view from the top," replied Srini. Raju could not make out who spoke as he was seeing multiple visions at that particular moment. Despite his inebriated state, he was adamant at not allowing anyone to go to the terrace.

"You need to leave now. Or I will have to inform the Principal," ordered Raju.

"Please Sir. We came here hoping to see the view. I was told by someone that Raju is a big-hearted person and he will allow us to go to the terrace," cajoled Srini.

"How do you know my name? And who are you?"

"You are very famous in college sir. I thought you were aware of that. I am Srini and these are my friends - Sivu, Vishu and Avi."

Raju took a few minutes to process the information. He continuously stared at Srini wondering if Srini was lying. Before he could say something, it seemed as if Srini had read his mind and spoke, "I am not lying. You can ask others if you want. If you do not allow us then you will be proving everyone who praised you wrong. I promise that we will not take more than a few minutes at the top."

Raju did not budge and kept on staring at Srini without saying a word. But Srini was determined to get the access to the top by hook or crook. He quickly got some money out from his pocket and said, "I have also learnt that you occasionally prefer to drink alcohol. This is a small token of appreciation from the four of us."

Sivu whispered, "Occasionally?"

Srini nudged Sivu and mumbled, "Shut up! Will you?"

He offered the money to Raju and continued, "You should take this and have some good drink later in the evening. Please unlock the gate and let us in."

Raju was tempted after seeing the money in Srini's hand. He took the money and said, "Only five minutes. Get back by then!" He fumbled with the set of keys for few seconds before finding the right one for the lock. Once the gate was opened, Srini thanked him and all four climbed the stairs to the terrace.

"That was so lame. You did not even do the convincing job well," said Avi.

"As long as the work gets done, I don't care. Moreover, you should be happy that I got you all access to the top."

"There is a reason why we call you the boss," joked Vishu.

It was very windy at the terrace. The wind whistled through the railings at the top. "Someone hold Vishu or he will fly away with the wind!" giggled Avi, taking a dig at Vishu's build. All of them went to the end of the stands facing the inner stadium and stood by the railings. The stunning view from the top left them momentarily speechless as they drank in the vastness of the college. The panoramic view included the tracks, goal posts, green field at the center, stands, podium, DCE admission building, open-air theater, entrance gate, hostels and department buildings. They were able to see most of the buildings in DCE from the top.

"Wow! This is so amazing," exclaimed Avi, "I have never seen anything like this before." He continued in his poetic style,

"Brilliant would be an understatement for this sight,

A perfect blend of scene and light;

If not for the fear of flunking,

I would definitely end up here every day, classes bunking."

"Neither have I. This is surreal. I am dumbstruck," uttered Sivu.

"Superb. I like this place. I wish we could spend more time here. We need to go down ASAP or that security guard will come chasing us," groaned Vishu.

"Forget it; let's spend some more time here. I am quite sure Raju would have fallen asleep somewhere in the stadium. He was totally drunk and was barely able to stand," assured Srini.

"Awesome. Let's look around then," said Avi, "I am really excited to see what else we have on the terrace."

"Nothing much except for the breathtaking view. There is one more thing that we must see. Actually, the whole purpose of getting you all here was to show you guys something else apart from the view. Come with me." Srini guided them a little further away from the staircase and the others followed him curiously. A few feet ahead, they were blinded because of the sudden glare of the sunlight reflected from large glass-like sheets placed in a uniform manner. These sheets were present everywhere on the terrace, flat and facing the sun.

"I can barely open my eyes. Do we need to go any further?" asked Vishu.

"This is what I wanted you to see. This glass right here is the solar panel. We have a solar panel farm running all through the stadium terrace. Ours is the only college in Bangalore that is self-sufficient in terms of power. In fact, we transmit the extra power generated for others to consume."

Vishu and the others stood there looking at the solar panels, appreciating the technology their college had been using.

"I had come here once during the early days of college. I wanted to see each and every place in the college and I stumbled upon this place accidentally. Today, when you mentioned about your solar panel idea, I thought that you might want to see this."

"Wow! This is fabulous." Vishu's voice became soft.

"Don't drag yourself down. My whole intention was to show the existing technology and not to prove you wrong. Cheer up!"

"No! No! I am not feeling bad. I was thinking how foolish I was for not thinking of the terrace as an ideal place for this solar panel. They don't take up any useable real estate. I was suggesting that these panels could cover an entire land or field. How much more stupid can you get?" Everybody burst out laughing. They walked towards the railing and sat admiring the view.

"We are glad that you did not feel bad. You took it in the right spirit!" said Avi.

"There is no point in feeling bad about it. On the contrary, I am happy because I was on the right track. The problem was that I was behind time. If not this, some other idea will click."

"That's cool. All is fine then!" Avi turned around from Vishu and faced the view. "I cannot get enough of this view from here. I wish I had this view from the backyard of my house. This is mesmerizing!"

"It is good to enjoy this kind of view once in a while. Seeing it every day might not make it special like you guys are feeling now," Vishu continued, "You know what? It just struck me that this is a nice spot to bring Akhila too. I will definitely bring her sometime and I am sure that she will be thrilled."

No one else responded to Vishu's reply. They continued gazing at the view in front of them. "Oh that reminds me. Akhila wanted to meet all of you. I have been asking you a couple of times and it is not falling in place. Let me know when can you guys meet her."

"Err… Soon. Let's meet for sure," said Sivu.

"Soon? When exactly? How about in an hour or so? It is already late afternoon and she will be meeting me at the Katte in the evening. We could catch up then."

"Hmm. Let's see. We can meet her sometime later, too," replied Avi.

"You guys keep saying this every time. I didn't know that my friends were so busy that they couldn't meet my girlfriend even once!" Avi looked at Srini and Sivu for a moment. Vishu was quick enough to notice their expressions.

"What is going on? Is something wrong? Tell me," pleaded Vishu.

"Nothing Vishu. You are just thinking too much," said Srini.

"Am I? There is something wrong and I want to know what it is. You are hiding something from me. It has to do with Akhila and I want to know what it is."

"Not really. Trust me," said Srini.

"Don't take me for a fool here. I have noticed how you guys have been reacting and your glances whenever I speak about her. I know for sure that there is some issue. Come on now, tell me!" Vishu shouted. He was furious as the friends with whom he shared everything were hiding something from him. He stood up and was waiting for an explanation.

"All right! Err… Sivu, why don't you tell him?" suggested Avi.

"Why me? Srini, you are the boss. You should tell him."

"Cut the crap, guys. I am really serious here. Srini, you tell me. Now!" Vishu was losing his temper because of his friends' frivolous responses.

"Okay. Relax. Sit down patiently and then I will be able to tell you," assured Srini. Vishu sat down but his anger did not subside. He was breathing heavily and staring at Srini with his eyes wide open. Srini was not really prepared for this kind of situation and his other two friends had forcefully put him on a spot. He took a couple of minutes to think everything through before he opened his mouth.

"Listen. We heard something about Akhila from her friends. Apparently, she has been known to go around with guys and then dump them after a couple of months. We feel that she is not serious about you, either. She will not hesitate to dump you when the time comes. You need to know that we care for you and we do not want you to get hurt. It will be good if you seriously think about your relationship with her and…"

"Stop. You are badmouthing my girlfriend. I know her very well and she is not the kind of girl who will dump me and leave. As for her past, I do not care about what she has done. As long as our relationship is going well, I do not want to think of anything else."

"How do you know that she will not dump you tomorrow for some other guy? You need to understand that we are trying to help you," argued Avi.

"I know what this is all about. This is about me not spending more time with you guys. If I break up with her then I will come back to you. You are jealous of my girlfriend," shouted Vishu. He stood up and his temper seemed uncontrollable. The others stood up and tried to pacify him.

"Why would I be jealous of your girlfriend?" questioned Sivu. "I mean, I have a girlfriend and I don't have to be jealous about my friend's girlfriend."

"I don't even know why you are acting this way. I am surprised that you are supporting them."

"Look! No one is jealous of anybody here. It is for your own good that we are telling you to think things through. We just don't want you to regret in the future," assured Sivu.

Vishu started walking away at a brisk pace. He thought that there was no point in continuing the discussion any further. He felt like his close friends had let him down and he decided never to talk to them again. "Aathura gararige buddhi matta" and translates to mean, 'Don't do anything in haste. It will only harm you'," said Sivu.

"Stop Vishu. Talk to us," said Srini.

Vishu stopped and turned around. His eyes were wet and his voice had become shaky. He brought words forth with difficulty, "I don't think I want to meet you guys anymore. Good Bye!"

He strode away, down the stairs and through the stands. He could hear his friends calling his name and telling him to stop. But he kept on going and didn't stop till he was out of the college.

CHAPTER 7

He ran till his legs started to ache. He came to a halt in front of the Bugle Rock Park, a few hundred meters away from the college. He was panting and desperately wanted water. There was a water fountain inside the park for visitors to drink from and he rushed towards it. He was gasping for breath and trying to hold back his tears and as soon as he took some water in his mouth, his throat seized up and he began choking. Vishu splashed water on his face to hide his tears and decided to go to the top of the Bugle Rock. Vishu had come to this park numerous times with Akhila. His favorite spot was the watchtower, where he would sit by Akhila's side, holding her hand and admiring the view. Today, he was in no mood to see the view nor appreciate it. He was shattered by his friends' remarks and allegations against the girl he loved the most. His mind was torn apart from two sides, one side where his best friends with whom he had countless joyous moments; other side was the girl of his dreams with whom he had already planned his life. He could not imagine living happily without either of them and there was no question of picking a side. He sat at the watchtower and recollected happier moments with his friends. One such incident was the day of the peanut festival called Kadlekai Parishe", celebrated every year at Bull Temple road.

"Guys, let's go to the festival," said Vishu.

"What do we do over there? It is not meant for us," replied Srini.

"How do you know it is not for us? People from different places take part in this festival. At least we will have peanuts to munch on."

"Yeah. Come on then! We shall check it out," jumped Avi excitedly.

They left the college campus and walked towards the Bull Temple road. There were carts and stalls everywhere. Most of them were peanut stalls although a few stalls sold sweets, balloons and trinkets. The road was heavily secured with barricades to keep vehicles at bay. Only pedestrians were allowed to cross the barricade and enjoy the festival. The guys stood near the barricade for few minutes looking around and observing the people at the festival. Many vendors had heaps of peanuts in each of their respective stalls. As the name of the festival indicated, it looked like a sea of peanuts. The farmers in and around Bangalore had brought truckloads of peanuts to sell at the festival. All four of them were mesmerized looking at what lay ahead of them. They hopped from one stall to other looking at the items on display. The smell of hot jalebis pulled the guys towards the sweet stall. The vendor was preparing jalebis afresh and a batch of jalebis, taken right out of the hot sugar syrup, got sold out in no time. The guys could not resist the sight of the fresh, bright orange and hot jalebis anymore. They convinced Vishu to get few from the vendor. Munching on the delicious jalebis, they moved on to other stalls.

Avi was attracted towards the robots that could predict the future in one of the stalls. He wanted to try them out. "Future predicting robot! How cool is that? Who is with me for that one?"

"Do you really think that the robot knows something you don't?" said Srini in a sarcastic tone.

"I know, I know! I am trying it because it seems fun."

"You give me the same amount and I will predict your future for you," joked Vishu.

Avi did not listen to anyone and went to the clairvoyant robot to know his future. He paid the money to the vendor and wore the headphones. He punched in his date of birth and started listening to what the robot had to say. His friends stood beside him till he was done knowing his future. A couple of minutes later, he returned the headphones and started cursing the robot. Apparently, the clairvoyant robot had mentioned the generic characteristics of his star sign. While the other three friends could not control their laughter, Avi was furious and moved on to the other stalls. Further ahead, they passed a cotton candy vendor and Sivu was tempted. He forced Vishu, who grudgingly agreed to his request to get the candy for him. They reached the entrance of the Bugle Rock Park. Before entering the park, Srini forced Vishu to buy some peanuts.

"I am not going to get anything this time. I have gone twice already: once to get you jalebis and again to get you cotton candy!"

"This will be the last time. Get the peanuts and join us in the park. Get the roasted ones." Vishu grumbled under his breath and went to the vendor closest to the entrance of the park. Soon, he returned with four packets of peanuts and handed three to his friends. He walked ahead while the rest of them opened their packets.

"Hey! This has only the shells. Where are the peanuts?" quipped Sivu after running his hand through the packet.

"Same here!"

"Even mine," shouted the other two guys.

Vishu was a couple of steps ahead of them and he turned around, "Really? Strange! I have the peanuts in mine." He started laughing at them as he had filled the other three packets with peanut shells and handed to them.

"Catch him. Bugger!" exclaimed Srini. Vishu had started running before the others decided to run after him. They followed him and Avi was catching up. They ran through the crowded place squeezing between the pedestrians and making their way. Vishu ran to the top of the rock, close to the watchtower and the others followed. When there was no other way to run down from the top, the others gathered around him and started throwing the peanuts shells at him. Vishu started to laugh and eventually all of them joined in as they sat down for some time.

◄►❖◄►

A bird chirping in the distance brought back Vishu to reality. The sun had already set and it was getting darker. There was no sign of the moon yet. The sky was dull, just like Vishu's mood at that moment. He was sitting at the same place where once he had laughed with his close friends. Today, he had no one around him. He sat there for some more time going over the events of the afternoon. He realized that he had been hasty and he had not given his friends a chance to explain what they really meant. He felt miserable for how he had reacted. He felt like meeting them and apologizing in person. One thing he knew for sure was that his friends would definitely forgive his mistake and get along just like before. He got up and slowly dragged himself home. Once there, he was in no mood for dinner. With the thought of his friends and the worry of how he would approach them looming over his head, he fell asleep immediately. The next day, he got up early and left home soon. He ran towards the

Katte once he reached the campus. No one was around as he had reached very early. As he waited for them a bundle of nervous energy balled up in his stomach. Hundreds of students passed by but his friends did not turn up. Vishu decided to go to the place where he had met them last. He reached the stadium stands huffing and panting. He took the stairs to the terrace, as the gate was still unlocked. He looked around the terrace and no one was there either.

He came out of the stadium and headed towards the department. On his way, he checked the cafeteria and the coffee kiosks. Inside the department, he searched the classrooms hoping that they would be in them. They were not in the classroom either. He headed towards the lab and they weren't there, either. He frantically searched every block including the library, admission building, open-air theatre and auditorium. They were nowhere to be seen. Tired and exhausted, he returned to the Katte. A few students were sitting on the Katte but none of them were his friends. He started getting impatient. He didn't know what to do next. He sat on the Katte for the next couple of hours eagerly waiting for his friends to arrive. None of them turned up.

"Hey Vishu! Where have you been since yesterday?" It was Akhila's voice. For once, he wanted it to be the voice of one of his friends. She came and sat down beside him. He poured his heart out to her. Being an understanding friend, she made up her mind to help him disregarding the fact that his friends had spoken ill of her. Vishu told her that he had searched for them in every nook and corner of the college and they were not there. "Do you know their phone numbers? We could call them and check."

"None of us use cell phones and you know that."

"Hmm… Let's go to their rooms and find out."

"I did go to the hostel dorms. I didn't see any of them there."

"Let's wait for a day. I am sure they would have bunked the classes today and gone out somewhere. You can meet them tomorrow once they return to college."

"They will be okay right?" said an extremely concerned Vishu.

"I am sure. Let's go home today and meet them tomorrow. Come now," she consoled Vishu as a parent would console a child.

"I shouldn't have fought with them in the first place. This is all my mistake."

"That's alright! I am sure they will understand." Akhila walked him home and promised to meet him at the Katte early next morning. She bid him goodbye after cheering him up a little bit and proceeded to her dorm. The following day was no different compared to the previous one. Vishu sat at the Katte with Akhila and waited for his friends to stop by. She was consoling him every now and then that they would come anytime soon. There was no sign of them till late afternoon. He became anxious and pestered Akhila about what to do next.

"Akhila, they are not here yet. What should we do?" She was in a deep thought and was not listening to him. "Akhila! Akhila! Where are you lost?"

"I read an article a week ago in the newspaper. I was thinking about that."

"What was that article about?"

"Never mind. It is not worth mentioning."

"No! Do tell me! Please. If it helps in finding my friends then I want to know."

"Vishu, I don't think it is an article which will help in anyway. So, just leave it."

"Tell me. Will You?"

"Okay. Promise me that you won't panic."

"Yes, I won't."

"So, recently in the city, there have been many kidnapping cases of teenagers, especially students from colleges, being reported. These kidnapping cases are apparently not for ransom. The Police suspect human trafficking. They think that the kidnapped students are sold to other countries for forced labor. The number of people missing in the past two months has been noticeably high. There are no clues about the person behind all these cases or the country to which the kidnapped students are being sold. The Police also suspect that there is a highly influential person behind all these wrong doings. Hence, that person is able to cover all his tracks and get away every time."

"My friends got kidnapped? That is why they are not in college. They got kidnapped! They got kidnapped!" shouted Vishu. He could not control himself after hearing about the article.

"No, Vishu. We don't know anything yet. It is just a hunch and we can't come to any conclusion yet. All I was thinking of was that we should give a Police complaint."

"Police? Why Police?" He was in such a state of shock that he did not know what he was saying.

"So that they can find out where your friends are. We can get to them faster."

After few moments of silence, he spoke, "Do you really think so?"

"I do. No harm in giving a complaint."

"Will you come with me to give a complaint? I want to go now. They better find my friends soon."

She agreed to come along and they headed towards the Police Station in Basavangudi. This was located behind the Bugle Rock Park. They walked to the Police Station and it took a few minutes to reach. It was a fairly old building adjoining a playground field. There were a lot of bikes and cars parked in front of the Station. These were vehicles the authorities had towed away from the no parking zones or from accident scenes. They reached the Station and Vishu stopped in front of it. He stood there and started staring at the signboard. Akhila held his hands and reassured him that everything would be just fine. She took him inside the building. A few constables were standing outside the building and chatting. They looked up and gave Vishu and Akhila a good stare. However, they got back to their discussion. Both of them entered the building. There was a big hall with many people sitting at desks. At one end of the hall were the prisoner cells. Vishu and Akhila looked at the cells and quickly turned around to face a cop sitting at a desk near the entrance.

"What do you want?" asked the cop in a gruff voice.

"I need to give a complaint," stammered Vishu.

"Against whom?"

"Err... I don't know."

Vishu's reply ticked off the cop and he raised his voice, "What is this regarding?"

"My friends are missing. I need to find them."

"Oh! Missing case. Go to that cop and give the complaint," replied the cop pointing to another officer seated at the opposite desk. They went to the other cop's table and Vishu noticed the plaque at his desk which read 'Sub-inspector'.

"What?" This guy was ruder than the first cop.

"My friends! They have been missing since yesterday."

"How many of them?"

"Three friends. My batch mates... from college." The Sub-inspector took out a book and started scribbling something before he proceeded with his series of questions.

"Your name?"

"Vishu."

"Full name?" he growled.

"Vishwas Rana."

"Which college?"

"DCE. Next block from here."

"Tell me your address and contact number." He wrote the address on the complaint sheet and proceeded to fill other standard sections.

"Your friends. Tell me their names."

"Srini, Sivu and Avi."

"Not like this. You need to provide full names of each guy and details about them."

Vishu provided the names and details of his friends. The Sub-inspector noticed that all of them did not have cell phones. "Don't you guys use cell phones? Surprising. Cell phones have spoilt the younger generation. You can't live without phones. In our days, we did not have a landline connection in our neighbourhood!" grumbled the Sub-inspector. "By the way, have you brought any photographs of these guys?"

"No! I haven't got any!"

The Sub-inspector filled up few more sections in the sheet and then he looked up, "When was the last time you met them?" As Vishu explained, the Sub-inspector leaned back in his chair. He seemed disinterested in Vishu's explanation.

"At the college stadium. Two days ago! I fought with them over some issue and left the place. I have been trying to find them after that altercation. I don't know where they have gone."

"Hmm…. Did you say you fought with them? What was the issue?" the Sub-inspector yawned in between asking questions and that annoyed Vishu but he was helpless.

"Err… Ah… It was about my. friend… Akhila," Vishu introduced Akhila to him and continued, "They bad-mouthed her. I couldn't bear to hear anything wrong about her so I walked away leaving them behind."

"Why should that bother you? Is she your girlfriend?"

Vishu got bit annoyed and replied, "Sir, I do not think that it is something you need to know. It is a personal thing and moreover, it is not related to the case."

The Sub-inspector got angry by this straightforward reply. He was not used to people speaking in this tone with him. He retaliated with a gruff tone, "Don't try to teach me what to do and what to ask. I will decide what details are relevant to the case. All you need to do is reply to what is asked. If I ask you if she is your girlfriend, just answer to that. You understand?"

Vishu was getting flustered. He replied angrily, "What the hell? I do not think you have the right to ask such absurd questions."

At this point, the Sub-inspector lost his temper. "Absurd? Are you telling me that what I speak is rubbish?

Do you have any idea what I can do to you? I can arrest you for insulting an officer right away. Better yet, I can make it look like you harmed your friends because they abused your girlfriend!" He emphasized the word 'girlfriend' with air quotes. His tone got quite threatening and at this point, Vishu was intimidated.

"Sir! This is not how you treat people who come asking for your help. If you start threatening people like this then they will lose their faith in the Police. Try to understand that and speak politely. He is not able to find his friends and on top of that, you are troubling him. This is not how you treat people. I expect you to be more courteous here," shouted Akhila. From the beginning, she had been listening to the conversation without interrupting and when it went beyond a certain point she could not resist retaliating any longer. Everyone in the room turned around to look at the commotion going on at the Sub-inspector's table. They were amused to see someone venting their anger at the Sub-inspector.

"Madam! Please calm down. Please!" He was embarrassed and wanted to bring the situation under control.

"What is going on here?" The Inspector in the cabin next door came out to investigate the source of the commotion outside. The Sub-inspector stood up and saluted him. He said that it was a case of missing people and that he had everything under control.

"Excuse me, Sir! The Sub-inspector is threatening us instead of taking down the complaint. He is treating us like criminals," blurted out Akhila.

"My friends are missing, Sir! He is threatening me with false accusations," added Vishu.

The Inspector seemed to understand the situation. He went to the Sub-inspector and started yelling at him. "Are you out of your mind? We are the protectors of the citizens. We need to help them out when they approach us. You are scaring them. They will lose faith in us. Try to be courteous to everyone."

"Sir, I was just noting down their complaint and nothing …"

"I know exactly what you were doing. Give me the complaint!" He took the complaint book and headed towards his cabin. He asked Vishu and Akhila to follow him.

"Please take a seat. I am Aditya Shetty, Inspector of Basavangudi Police Station."

Aditya Shetty was a smart young man compared to the other cops in the former room. He was recently promoted to the post of Inspector after clearing a few exams. Unlike the Sub-inspectors, he was fit and apt for his role. He seemed to be understanding and was a good listener - he had two very important traits necessary for his profession. After Vishu and Akhila introduced themselves, the Inspector began skimming through the complaint.

⊷⋑◆⋐⊶

The Inspector spent a few more minutes scanning the complaint. The constable came inside to clear the teacups and the empty biscuit plate from the table. While he listened to Vishu's story, the Inspector had munched on all the biscuits, some of which were meant for the other two as well.

"So, did you check at your friends' homes?" questioned the Inspector.

"I did go to the hostel. They were not over there. We have always met at the college parking lot and I waited for two days before coming here."

"Do you have any photographs of your friends handy?"

"No. It didn't strike me. Even the Sub-inspector asked for one. We came directly from college."

"Don't worry. Let's go to your college and get the details from the students' records."

"But it will be closed now. It's evening already."

"No problem. I will get it opened for us. As a part of the Police force, we have the authority to investigate at any time or any place. Let's go. Moreover, your college is on the way to where I live and I was just about to head home."

Vishu jumped with relief. "Yes, Sir! Let's go."

Vishu and Akhila got up and headed towards the cabin's exit. The Inspector took his cap and baton before leaving his cabin. He followed the other two and came to the hall. The Sub-inspector stood up and saluted him.

"I am heading towards Vishu's college now. I will be away for some time."

"I can join you, Sir!"

"No need. I will take someone else along with me. You stay here."

"Okay, Sir!"

"And be courteous to people who come. Don't forget!"

"Yes, Sir!"

Aditya Shetty recruited one of the constables to accompany them to the college. They headed towards the jeep that was waiting outside the Police Station. The driver was ready and he started the engine. Everyone hopped into the jeep and proceeded towards DCE.

CHAPTER 8

The Inspector sat along with the driver in the front seat and the others hopped into the back seats of the jeep. The sun was about to set and the sky had turned into an ominous shade of reddish orange. There were a few dark clouds here and there hinting at the possibility of a drizzle sooner or later. The driver turned on the headlights and cranked up the engine. The jeep seemed to be quite old despite being well maintained. It came to life after two cranks and roared as the driver pressed the accelerator pedal. The driver left the station compound and continued on the main road toward the college. The Inspector turned around and faced Akhila. "Do you know his friends well?"

"No. In fact, I haven't even met them in person." Akhila replied in a cold tone. She was still trying to digest the fact that his friends had bad-mouthed her.

"Please, don't hold a grudge against them Akhila. This is not the time," pleaded Vishu.

"Well, that's the truth. I have never met them formally nor have I spoken to them. I have only seen his group sitting on the Katte. But I have heard a lot about them from Vishu."

"That is okay. You will get to meet once we find them," assured the Inspector.

"I hope so." She wore a stern expression on her face. It looked like she was trying to avoid Vishu's eyes. She was not sure if she wanted to meet them after this episode. On one hand, she was sad about Vishu's anxiety and hoped that things would work out fine between him and his friends. On the other hand, she was still sore at the remarks that his friends had made about her. Though she had not brought this up with Vishu, she wanted to clarify things with him and his friends at some point. For now, nothing mattered more than finding them safe and sound.

They reached the college campus within a few minutes. The gate was latched and that prompted the driver to honk. A visibly disgruntled security guard came from his watchtower and opened the gate. His annoyed look soon gave way to fear when he saw the word 'POLICE' written in bold on the windshield. He opened the gate wide open and the vehicle came to a halt in front of the admissions building. It was dark by then and there were hardly any students out in the campus. Most of them were done with their classes and had left the campus. The ones who were present were either loafing around or were practicing a sport. They were quite surprised to see a Police jeep enter the campus, that late in the evening. They looked at the Inspector, constable and the two students disembarking the jeep and wondered what the issue was. Vishu and the others headed towards the admissions office in the building. The long corridor was dimly lit and was empty. The entrance door to the office had a board saying "Admissions" hung on it. The Inspector directly barged in without knocking on the door. The rest obediently followed him into the office.

The man behind the counter was fumbling with a computer. The office was almost empty and the only sound was the one coming from the keyboard as he typed away furiously. The huge wooden cabinet behind him was open and contained dusty registers. He was seated on a wooden chair, which creaked as he shifted his weight. His table was full of open books. Crumpled papers surrounded the trash bin, all proof of an unorganized office. He stood up when he saw the Inspector. Vishu studied his face closely. He looked a little worked up initially, and after seeing Vishu walk in with the Inspector, he looked even more flustered.

"Oh. Hello. Is everything alright Sir?"

"What is your name? What do you do here?" the Inspector asked.

"I am Prasad, the night shift guy. I take care of the admin sundry work here. What have I done, Sir?"

"You don't need worry. I am here to get information about three students of this college. Can you pull up their files?"

Prasad was slightly relieved hearing this, "Sure Sir. I can do that for you. Please come inside."

As he moved to one of the desktop computers, the others crossed the counter and stood behind him. He logged into the college database by punching in his credentials. He hit the search button in order to get the details of the candidates. A window popped up asking for the name or the ID number of the student to retrieve the records. Vishu spelt out his friends' names for Prasad and he began searching for them one by one. The computer was an older model, which made the process slow. Vishu waited anxiously. He was comforted slightly by the fact that the Inspector was helping him out but little did he know that he was hovering between the frying pan and the fire.

"Sir, there are no records for these three students in here," Prasad declared.

Everyone stared at the computer screen that had popped up a window reading *ERROR: No record found.*

The Inspector growled, "Check again. There must be a mistake." Prasad was irked at being asked to search the system again. The same thing happened this time and he could not locate their records. He said rudely, "No use. I searched in front of you. You saw me type the whole thing."

"Then check for Vishu's name. Let's see if the system is working fine," ordered the Inspector.

After Vishu gave his full name, the system showed: "Vishwas Rana – First year Engineering – Computer Science. Search result: 1 record found."

"The system is working fine, Sir. But those students records do not exist," confirmed Prasad.

Vishu lost his temper, "How can you say this? I have been studying with them for over six months now. We have come to this college almost every day. And yet you are telling me that they do not exist in the system? I am sure you have done something." He turned to the Inspector and said, "Sir, I am sure he has been messing with the records. Take him away and ask him."

"Vishu. Calm down!" The Inspector said with a stern face, which immediately silenced everyone. Prasad's sudden change in tone had caught the Inspector off guard. Moreover, the office was in utter shambles and that was very suspicious. "Were you fiddling with the student records? It is quite uncommon for the office to be this messy, especially when it is the closing time. I think you are up to something. Tell me the truth or I will have to take you to the station for further questioning.

Prasad's face turned white on hearing this. He began stammering nervously, "S-s-sir, Trust me. I know n-n-nnothing about these students. This is the f-f-f-first time I ever heard those names. Sir, please. I do not know anything."

"Tell me the truth," the Inspector pressed him harder.

"I do not have the access to delete the records. I am telling you the truth Sir. I have acc-c-cess to only view the records. I c-c-c-cannot modify anything, Sir."

"Who has the access to modify the contents?"

"The Principal and his as-s-s-sistant staff. Only they can modify the records, Sir!"

"Is he here now? Can you call him?"

"Sir, he is not in Bangalore. He will be back in a couple of days. He has gone to attend a … "

Before he could finish, Vishu blurted out again, "Sir we cannot wait that long. They will harm my friends. Please do something."

"Vishu, stop interrupting. I understand that you are concerned. But let me do my job," the Inspector was annoyed. He turned to Prasad and said, "Give me the Principal's address and contact number. Are you sure there is nothing else going on here?" he removed his handcuffs from his belt and brandished it.

"Sir, I don't know anything else. I am just a night shift guy!" Prasad was close to crying and breaking down at this point.

"That's okay. Give me your address and contact details." The Inspector put his handcuffs back and took the details from Prasad. This is something he had learned from experience. People usually got nervous once they saw Police artifacts like guns and cuffs. He was just trying to flush details out of Prasad. They stepped out of the office. Once they reached the jeep, the Inspector said to the constable,

"I don't think he knows anything. However, keep an eye on him while I try to contact the Principal."

"Right, Sir! I will do that."

"I will drop you both home now. It is already late. I will see if I can get hold of Principal or his assistant. Let us meet here tomorrow morning and talk to others. We might get some leads on the case."

Vishu stood there next to the jeep without moving an inch. He did not want to rest until he met his friends. The Inspector held his shoulders and said, "Trust me, son! Everything will be fine and you will meet your friends. Now, go home and take some rest. Understood?"

He nodded and did not say anything. "Also, be safe and stay indoors. The students' records going missing from the college database indicates that there might be bigger things happening. It might involve more people than we had thought initially."

"I understand, Sir!"

The Inspector dropped Akhila at the hostel and Vishu at home before heading towards the Police Station. It was a long night for Vishu and he sat on a table by the window, staring at the sky. He tried to connect the stars with imaginary lines and suddenly, he could see the faces of his friends in the stars. He loved creating images in the stars. There was no limit to the number of images that could come out of stars. They were as endless as the sky above him. He sat there for couple of hours in the same posture gazing at the sky through his open window. The cool breeze outside along with swooshing sound made by the trees outside made for a perfect night, neither too cold nor hot. In the middle of the night, he heard a few footsteps outside his house and after a while, he could hear insistent thumping on the front door.

The sound got louder and it sounded like the people outside were trying to break open the door. Vishu was concerned and was on the verge of getting scared. He cautiously peeped out of the window. He could not see anyone out there but the 'thud' sound was very distinctive. He realized that his front door had just one latch on it. He closed his bedroom door. Not knowing what else he could do, he hid himself in the cupboard. He was thinking of what could he do next and sat inside with his eyes closed to calm himself down.

'THUD!'

His bedroom door burst open. He tried very hard not to make a noise and muffled his mouth. He could see four-masked figures in his room through the crack in the door. They looked in his bed and upon not finding anyone in there, began looking around nervously. They spoke amongst themselves in a language that was foreign to Vishu. One of the guys was pointing at the open window and yelling something. He was able to understand their intent. That person must have been telling the others that Vishu might have run away through the window. These must be the same people who had kidnapped his friends. He cupped his mouth and sat silently. While he was thinking of how he would escape from them, one of the thugs walked towards the cupboard. The thug flung the door open and dragged him out. Vishu tried to escape from the clutches of the thug but the other three pounced on him making it impossible to get away. The first thing they did was to gag his mouth so that he could not scream. Vishu resisted, but was easily overpowered by four men. They kicked him with their heavy boots and dragged him out of the house. They had a white van parked in front of the house. The van had a huge trailer attached to it and it looked like a vehicle used for camping.

They threw him inside. They held him and tied his hands and legs.

"You pesky rat! How dare you give a complaint against our Boss? You will face the same consequences as your friends. Wait and watch," yelled one of the thugs. Everyone got in the van and one of the thugs slammed the door. The van started to move and Vishu was jostled around as the van picked up considerable speed.

He had no idea where was he being taken. For a moment, Vishu thought that he might finally be reunited with his friends. But the thought was immediately overshadowed by fear. What if they harmed him and his friends together? He could hear them talking to someone on a cell phone and presumed that they were getting instructions from the caller who was their Boss. Vishu wondered if he could get a hold of the details of the Boss and then he would be able to get his friends back by informing the Inspector. The thought gave him strength. But for all that, he would need to escape from the van. He began kicking the door from inside even though his legs were tied. He was barefoot, so each kick was painful. But the door did not budge. Vishu did not care. The sound from kicking the door was masked by the noise from the engine. He kicked harder. The door seemed to have loosened as he could feel the wind on his neck. He mustered all his strength and kicked it one more time. Before he could realize what was happening, he was thrown out of the car.

He fell on the ground with a thud. He screamed out of pain and opened his eyes. To his surprise, he was still at home and had fallen from the table on which he was sitting. He had dozed off on the table and had a nightmare about the kidnappers. He was relieved to know that he was still at home and not on the road with his hands and legs tied. The relief, however, lasted for a moment, before reality came crushing back upon him. He remembered the current situation and pined for his missing friends. More than anything, his helplessness was hurting him the most. He had no idea of his friends' whereabouts. He was counting every minute left for the break of the dawn so that he could reach college and wait for the Inspector. The Inspector was his only hope. He wanted the investigation to end soon and get his friends back from the kidnappers. The rooster's crow in the morning woke him up. He had hardly slept for a couple of hours. He dressed up quickly and had some light breakfast before stepping out of the house. He was eagerly waiting to hear updates from the Inspector. He wanted to know if he had met the Principal, if he gotten a lead on the culprits. More importantly, he just wanted to hear that his friends were safe. He reached college a bit earlier than he intended to. Akhila had agreed to meet them but she had not turned up yet. He went and sat on the Katte making sure that he had a complete view of the parking lot.

Inspector Aditya Shetty arrived with the constable. As Vishu looked at them getting down from the jeep, Akhila walked into the parking lot. The sight of Akhila brought a fleeting moment of joy to him. The Inspector greeted Akhila and they walked together towards him.

"Sir, were you able to speak to the Principal?"

"No. I was not able to reach him on phone. Let's wait and meet him in person. Meanwhile, shall we talk to few people on campus who may have seen your friends?"

"Sure Sir. Let's do that. I know a few people who knew them."

"So, tell me again when did you last meet them? Do you remember the last person all of you spoke to? Any suspects?"

"Yes, of course. It was the security guard, Raju, at the stadium. We ran into him while we were on our way to the terrace. He was the last person who had seen us together."

"Perfect! Let's head to the stadium then." All of them walked towards the stadium. A few minutes later, they entered the archway and reached the field. Vishu started shouting the guard's name and after couple of seconds, Raju responded. He was on the podium and came running towards them seeing the Police. He stopped right in front of the Inspector and saluted him.

"Are you Raju, the security guard?"

Raju was already shivering with fear. "I have not done anything, Sir."

"Are you Raju?" the Inspector asked again, with a louder tone.

"Yes Sir. I am Raju."

"Did you meet this boy and his friends a few days ago in the stadium?"

"Him?" he looked at Vishu with a puzzled look.

"Sivu, Avi, Srini and I were here and you let us go to the terrace. Don't you remember? Srini even gave you some money for your drinks."

He was embarrassed remembering that had taken a bribe from the students. It was as if the mention of the word 'money' brought back his memory and he said, "Yes Sir. I saw them here. I let them go to the top."

"Do you know what happened after that?"

"I don't know Sir. They went upstairs and I didn't follow them. I had some work in the stadium."

"Did you see them leave the stadium? Did you see anyone else apart from these four that day?"

"I was not around. I let them in and went ahead with my work. I don't know what they did up there. I did not see them leaving either."

The Inspector asked Vishu to take him to the spot where Vishu had spent time with his friends the last time he was there. Nodding, Vishu led him to the terrace and explained why Srini had gotten everyone there in the first place. He showed the Inspector the solar cells and the college view they were admiring just before the fight started.

After hearing the story patiently from Vishu, the Inspector strolled around the place and looked around. He took a closer look at the solar panels and the aisle way beside them. He was about to walk away to the group standing at the entrance of the terrace when he noticed sunlight reflecting from a glass piece near the solar panel. He bent down to pick up the piece and soon realized that it was a broken piece from a spectacle frame. A little further ahead, he noticed a small red stick lying beside the parapet wall. The red stick was actually part of the spectacle frame, which only had one intact glass. He picked up the frame and approached Vishu, "Do you remember whose spectacles these are?"

Vishu was surprised. "Oh, this is Sivu's. He was near sighted and this was his new pair of glasses."

The Inspector turned towards the constable and said, "Take this and send it to the lab. See if we can find some fingerprints on it." He looked at Raju and in a raised voice asked, "Do you still say that you didn't see them leaving the building? Don't lie to me." Raju was terrified and started to shiver in fear. In broken language, he said he did not know anything about their whereabouts.

"You need to come to the Police Station later and give these details in writing. If you remember anything unusual from around that time, let us know immediately."

"Okay, sir. I will," replied Raju hesitantly.

While leaving the stadium, the Inspector told the constable, "It is strange that three students went missing without anyone noticing, especially the security guard. He might be hiding some vital information. Keep an eye on him." The constable nodded in agreement. They left the stadium and walked towards the Katte. They passed the admissions office and Vishu was reminded of the fact that his friends' records were missing. He said, "How can they let this happen? Can't they make their system secure? Things like these spoil the reputation of the college."

"Vishu, it is not the college's fault. If someone is up to no good, they will not stop at anything to cover their tracks. We might be dealing with some very smart people here. We need to get to the bottom of the case to find out who is behind all these. I wonder how many other cases like this have gone unnoticed without anyone reporting," said the Inspector worrying about the missing teens. "Whom do we talk to next?"

Just then, someone called out Vishu's name from behind. They turned around to see Professor Ravi Nagraj walking towards them. "Vishu, what are you doing here? I did not see you in my class yesterday!" Vishu remembered the incident when he was in Professor Nagraj's class and how he had managed to embarrass himself in front of everybody. Not only was he caught sleeping in class but he had walked out of the class as well later.

"Hello, Professor. Sorry for missing your class. We are in big trouble!" Turning to the Inspector, he introduced him.

"This is Inspector Aditya Shetty. We are looking for my friends Avi, Srini and Sivu. They have been missing for the last couple of days."

"Oh! I am sorry to hear that. How did that happen? I hope they are alright!" The Professor seemed agitated after hearing the news about his students being missing. His face shrank and a flood of thoughts came to his mind all at once.

"We are still trying to figure out how they went missing. The Inspector has given us a lot of support."

"Don't worry about class!" He turned to the Inspector, "Is there any way I can help?" the Professor was concerned upon hearing this.

"Vishu tells me that they sat in class together all the time. Do you remember seeing any of them in the campus in the last two days?

"Hmm…" the Professor pondered for a while. "The names do sound familiar. However, I am not able to put a face to them."

"Professor, don't you remember the day when you had asked me who the father of C was? I did not answer and you yelled at me. After that I walked out of your class. My friends were sitting beside me."

"Ah yes. I remember that day. You were sleeping. I have seen a couple of students sitting around him. But I do not remember their faces. I see so many students every day and I often mix up faces. Pardon me. I am very bad at it."

"That's alright, Professor."

"Is there anything else I can assist you with? If not, I have to rush to a class now. I guess I am already late."

"No problem. Carry on. I appreciate your time."

"My best wishes. I hope they find your friends soon." The Professor turned around and headed back into the department.

The Inspector turned to Vishu and asked him, "So, who should we speak to next?" Vishu replied, "Let's go to our department." They headed towards the Computer Science block and went to the first floor, which had the Professors' office. Vishu spotted lab instructor, Mrs. Jayashree Nath, in the corridor. He was reluctant to even approach her. They shared a bad rapport and for some reason Vishu always ended up in a situation where he would either get yelled at, or get thrown out of the lab. Normally, Vishu would never talk to her willingly, but this was the pursuit of his friends. So he was ready to ask her for help.

"Sir, the lady over there is our lab instructor. She stays in the lab all day. The lab is equipped with better computers and they are all plugged into the college network. Someone might have used these systems to hack into the database as well. Shall we go ask her to see if she has noticed anything different in particular?"

"Sure." They walked towards her and the Inspector greeted her.

"Good morning Madam, do you have a minute to spare?"

"Hello," Mrs. Jayashree looked at the Inspector. She gave Vishu a cold stare as though she had been expecting this day when he might be in big trouble. "What is the matter?"

The Inspector pointed at Vishu and asked her, "We are looking for his friends who have been missing for the past three days. Sivu, Srini and Avi. Do you remember seeing them in the lab anytime since then? Or has there been any unauthorized access to the lab computers?"

"I don't remember anyone by these names. You must be mistaken."

"Ma'am, we were in the same batch when you took our Viva the other day!" Vishu told, hoping that this might help Mrs. Jayashree remember something.

"All I remember that day is that you answered incorrectly. You were behaving very weird that day. I don't remember any Sivu or Avi or the third guy you mentioned in your batch. If you are done with your investigation, I have a class now," replied lab instructor with a cold expression. Seeing the Inspector nod, she walked away leaving the others dumbstruck in the corridor.

"I don't like this instructor. She hates me. She would never help me with anything. I was hoping that she would be a bit humane this time around. I guess I was wrong."

"Hmm... Why do you think she does not remember your friends? It looks like she is not too fond of you and your friends."

"Yes, we know. She always scolds us, me in particular, and there is a good chance that she would prefer us being missing than being in her lab."

"That's strange!" The Inspector said with his eyebrows arched. He peeped into the lab. A motley bunch of students were happily typing away on the computers. These systems looked better than the one they saw in the office. The Inspector made a mental note to come and look at the access logs of these computers later in the day. They walked out of the building and came to the garden in the front. As they proceeded towards the parking lot, Vishu saw his batch mate, Nitesh walking ahead of them. He quickly ran ahead yelled out at him, "Hey Nitesh. Got a minute?" Nitesh waved at

Vishu and walked towards him. "Hey, have you seen Srini, Sivu and Avi in the last couple of days?"

"Who are they? Are they from our batch?"

"Bugger! Stop kidding. Remember the time you invited me to the pub. We were sitting together near the katte that time!"

"Oh. The Katte is always crowded and I might have missed them. Maybe they are in some other department. Anyways, I was in a hurry that day and …"

By this time, the Inspector and his constable caught up to them. Seeing them, Nitesh got a bit intimidated. It was quite uncommon to see the police in the department corridor. He abruptly stopped. "Anyway, I do not remember seeing them that day. I am in a hurry. May I leave now?" The Inspector did not find anything suspicious in him and he allowed Nitesh to leave.

Vishu was surprised "That is weird. I don't know why he acted that way. Idiot."

"Okay Vishu. Whom do we meet next?" The inspector was getting irritated with the bunch of people Vishu was talking to. Vishu was about to say something when the bell rang indicating the end of the hour. The door of the classroom opened and a chattering bunch of students walked out the room towards the garden. These were the senior students of the college who were in their last year. Vishu immediately recognized these folks. Few of these students had ragged him during his initial days. The seniors just lingered around the Katte, looking for freshmen trying to catch them and make them do embarrassing things. The coursework for the last year was quite light and this prompted these seniors to hang out in the campus for the better part of the day. They knew most of the college staff by the end of the fourth year and thus they had an easy time wherever they went and got away with whatever they did.

"Sir. These students are our seniors. They hang around in the campus all day. They spend a lot of time in the parking lot usually. If anything suspicious has happened, they might have seen it. For all you know, they might have seen my friends. After all, they ragged us. Let's go talk to them." Vishu spotted the student who had ragged all four of his friends on their first day at DCE. He was walking towards the parking lot.

"Hey, you! Hey," shouted Vishu waving his hand as they walked towards him. The senior looked up and for a moment he could not recognize Vishu. "Hey, do you remember me? You were the one who ragged me and my friends on day one."

"Yeah. You complained to the Police regarding that? That was for fun man!" the senior looked concerned. The sight of cops and the mention of ragging got him worried.

"Hey no. Of course not! They are not here for that."

A little relieved, the senior asked, "Okay good. What do you want?"

Vishu continued, "Do you remember my other three friends from day one? Srini, Sivu and Avi?"

"I don't know who they are. In fact, I don't know many freshmen students. There is a new batch every year and we don't really get to know them. However, if you say they are your friends and that they were with you, I definitely don't want to know them." He replied, emphasizing the word 'your'. That caught the Inspector's attention and he asked, "Hey. What do you mean? What has Vishu done to you?"

"Why don't you ask him, Inspector? I don't want to be associated with him or any of his so-called friends. I have a class starting in ten and I need to grab some food by then.

With your permission Inspector, may I please leave now?" The Inspector decided there was no point in holding him back for any more time and let him go.

"I don't remember meeting him any other time except on day one. Why would he say that?" Vishu pondered loudly. "Here I am looking for my missing friends and people are choosing to be rude today of all days."

"Vishu, we need to hurry now. We haven't gotten any solid lead regarding your friends today. Let's get going. Where next?" The Inspector asked.

"It's almost noon. Shall we have lunch and then resume?" asked Akhila saying something after a long time. She was famished running around the campus and needed a break.

"We probably should take a break now," agreed Vishu hesitatingly. They decided to have a quick meal at the cafeteria before proceeding with meeting others.

CHAPTER 9

The cafeteria was the preferred hangout area for both students and faculty members mainly because of its proximity and the perks that the place offered. Although the food was not all that great, it was available at subsidized prices. Other than a few select occasions where students walked a few meters away from college for good food, they ended up going to the cafeteria regularly. Today, it was surprisingly less crowded even though it was the lunch hour at DCE. All four entered the cafeteria and except for the Inspector, the rest ordered food.

"I will stick to a cup of coffee. I had a heavy breakfast." The inspector took the coffee from the counter. Grabbing a chair at an empty table, he sat alone perusing the case file. While the others got their food and settled on another table, he started flipping through the pages and sipping his hot coffee. The case file had all the details of the case captured so far. He chose to begin with 'First Information Report' commonly known as the FIR. He skimmed through the FIR hoping to find some clue that would give him the answers he was looking for.

The FIR had Vishu's version of the story: the last seen location and time of the missing friends; their appearance and contact details; the altercation they had among themselves. The case file also had details of the investigation so far including – the fishy clerk at the admin office; Raju

– the inebriated security guard; the Principal who was yet to be contacted. He also recollected the incidents with the curt lab instructor and the senior student. He had no clarity or lead on the case so far except finding the Sivu's spectacle frame from the terrace. He could not figure out how they could simply vanish into thin air without anyone noticing. Before putting the case file aside, he opened first page of the FIR, which had the descriptions of the missing people. He read it again to make a mental note of them.

"Srinavas Wah, height 6', well built, beige skin color, black eyes."

"Siva Sharan, height 6'1", fair skin color, lean guy, black eyes."

"Avinash Swar, height 5'6", brown eyes, fair, lean, mole on the nose."

Once he finished reading the report, he stepped out of the cafeteria carrying his cell phone. Seeing the Inspector step out, Vishu got up pushing the half eaten plate aside and headed to the restroom. He sat down on one of the empty chairs once he came out of the restroom and shook his head in dejection. The Inspector had not finished his call yet and the rest of them sat in total silence engrossed in their own thoughts. Their silence was broken by the bark of a dog from outside. Vishu's face lit up at the sound of barking. He dashed out of the cafeteria to see Muffin near the Katte calling out for his master. He ran towards the dog even though he was not a lover of pets, in particular dogs. "Muffin! Over here! Muffin." The dog saw Vishu and came running to him. It seemed as if the dog had missed the whole group. Vishu petted the dog, as Avi would have done.

"Sir, this is muffin. Avi's pet dog! He used to pamper and feed him. He even taught him a trick or two."

The Inspector had finished his phone call and stood beside Vishu looking at the dog. He was amused to see Vishu hugging and playing with the dog, momentarily forgetting about his friends. Ever since the investigation began that morning, the Inspector saw that everything on the campus reminded Vishu of his friends and their fond memories. He was reminded again that he had not landed any concrete lead on the case so far and had to make some quick progress.

"Sir, I have an idea," Vishu got up while he continued speaking, "We can use the dog and find my friends. We can look for Avi if we find any of his clothes or his belongings for muffin to pick up the smell. Why didn't I think of this before?"

The Inspector and the constable burst out laughing. "We cannot use any dog to search for your friends. The dogs that the Police use to locate people are trained specifically for that purpose. I am afraid this dog won't be of any help to the case."

Vishu was disappointed. He sat there absentmindedly petting the dog. The Inspector sat down next to him and said, "I promised that I will find out the truth. Be patient and everything will be fine." After a pause, he continued, "I will be gone for a couple of hours now. Be here at the Katte and I will return soon."

Vishu nodded. Akhila stayed with him while the constable accompanied the Inspector and walked towards the Jeep. He continued petting the dog for a while and soon tired of it. He moved to an empty bench under the tree at the Katte. The dog followed him and sat beside his feet. All this while Akhila hardly spoke. She understood the situation and did not force him to talk either. Both looked tired and the cool shade under the tree was refreshing. Akhila opened a book and began reading through it. Vishu lied down on the bench and dozed off in no time. His sleep was broken by a screeching halt at the entrance of the parking lot. The Inspector had arrived. Vishu looked at his watch and realized he had slept for over an hour. The back door of the jeep flung open and he saw his friends getting down. They had returned safe and sound. They looked unharmed and were wearing exactly the same clothes he had last seen them in.

It was as if the floodgate of emotions had just been opened within Vishu. The onslaught of feelings however left him rooted to the spot. He saw his friends waving their hands and shouting his name from the distance. They were literally jumping for joy and it was evident that they were thrilled to be back in their college. Tears of joy rolled out of his eyes when he realized that they were all right. Three days of restlessness and exhaustion from running from pillar to post vanished in no time. He stood up, excited to welcome his friends back. He had loads of questions to ask – Who kidnapped them? Where they had been taken? Did the kidnappers harm them? How did they finally get out?

Before he could wave back, he saw somebody else running towards them from the Katte. That guy was waving and yelling their names at the top of his voice. His friends saw the guy and ran towards him. For a second, Vishu didn't understand why some other guy would run to embrace his friends. He could not understand why his friends as well were eager to meet someone else instead of him. He felt a pang of jealousy. He stood there feeling helpless and stared at them in disbelief. The other guy ran till he was near his friends. When he looked closely, Vishu was astonished to see that the guy who was running towards them looked exactly like him. He had the same build, height and hairstyle. He saw that his friends hugged the imposter thinking that he was Vishu. They jumped around and shouted at the top of their voices.

"A moment of happiness to relish,

A touch of friendship to believe;

A sight of togetherness to cherish,

A life of eternity to relive!" recited Avi.

A tap on Vishu's shoulder woke him up from his dream. It was the Inspector Aditya Shetty who had arrived with somebody else. Akhila had left to grab a cup of coffee from the nearby kiosk and she returned upon seeing the Inspector. Seeing Vishu lost in his deep thought, the Inspector had tapped him.

Vishu woke up and said, "I saw them, Sir. I saw them!"

"Who did you see, Vishu?"

"My friends! They got down from the jeep and they looked well. Interestingly, I saw myself going and hugging them. Everyone was happy, Sir. I saw my friends happy." Vishu gripped the Inspector's arm tightly and tried to convince him that he did indeed see his friends in good shape.

"You were dreaming Vishu. Calm down, we have work to do. By the way, meet my friend Mr. Ajay Kumar. He will accompany us henceforth." Vishu just smiled at Ajay and he did not even care to shake his hand. His mind was preoccupied with the dream and everything else at that point seemed irrelevant.

"Now, I want you to find another person who is a friend of either Srini, Sivu or Avi. Do you know anyone else who hangs out with any of them? One of your friends might have tried contacting that person."

"Hmm… Someone who knows one of my friends well!" Vishu could not think of any such person.

"Anyone who knows your friends individually. Any close friends, relatives or girlfriends?"

"Ah Yes! Of course! Sahana – Sivu's girlfriend. We can go find her."

"Where do you think we can find her? Do you have her contact number?"

"She is from a different department. All the students have probably left for the day. Else, we could have gone to her classroom block. No, I do not have her contact number. Only Sivu had it."

"Never mind. We can get the contact number or address from the Admissions Office." They headed towards the Admissions Office.

Akhila was excited to meet another girl who was a part of Vishu's friends' group. "I hope Sivu has tried reaching her. My instincts are saying that she will be of some help unlike the others."

"Women have powerful instincts. Let's see how it turns out," replied the Inspector. As they crossed the long corridor and came across the familiar 'Admissions Office' board outside the office, the Inspector noticed that the signboard 'Closed For Lunch' hung on the door. Being well aware of the inefficiencies of the administrative employees, the Inspector sighed looking at Akhila, "We have to wait for an hour or two to get the contact number. Maybe we will just end up meeting her tomorrow in class."

Akhila was not yet ready to give up. She turned to Vishu and asked, "Didn't Sivu mention that he met Sahana in the library quite often? We could try looking for her there."

"Good idea. The library is right across this building!" He pointed to the building in between the auditorium and the department blocks.

The Inspector and his group reluctantly agreed to proceed to the library, as this was the best shot they had at that moment. It was a small walk and they entered the library a few minutes later. The front desk had a computer for the students to scan their ID cards while entering and leaving the library. It also allowed students to check the status of the books that they came in search of. There was also a librarian seated at the front desk.

"We can look at the log in info to see if Sahana has checked in now. It would be easier to find out from here," Vishu suggested pointing to the front desk computer.

The Inspector sat in front of the computer and typed Sahana's name in the search field. The computer displayed an alert that said: "*Error: No records found. Please provide the ID in the search field!*"

"Looks like we cannot use the name to fetch the records. We need Sahana's ID to get the details. What do we do now?" the Inspector slammed his right fist on the desk wondering what their next move should be.

"How may I help you today, Inspector?" It was the librarian who had been busy doing some work until now behind the counter and he turned around listening to the commotion in front of the computer. He was a short stout guy with neatly combed hair. He was in his mid-forties, evident from the traces of grey in his hair. His desk behind the counter was spick and span and the documents on it were well organized. There was a metallic nameplate on his desk, which read, in bold letters: *Pradeep Shankar, Librarian*. He saw Vishu standing next to the Inspector and he gave him an accusatory stare, which quickly turned into an annoyed smirk. The Inspector said, "We are trying to see if a student has checked into the library. I tried typing the name in the search field and it said that the ID number is required to check information."

"I can help you with that. Administrative privileges allow me to search for students by name. We will be able to see all the check-in and check-out dates of the student so far."

"That is good. The student's name is Sahana. I do not think we know her last name," the Inspector said glancing at Vishu and Akhila, both nodded in affirmation.

"First name is fine. It might take longer to find out from the results as we do not have last name."

The librarian turned towards the computer on his desk and began working on it. Meanwhile, Ajay Kumar looked around the library. He noticed a café lounge adjacent to the main reading room. At the other end of the café was a long corridor that led to the silent room. The main reading room and the reception area had been renovated recently and state of the art equipment had been installed. He was surprised to see the CCTVs and the access control devices placed inside the library.

"You were lucky I guess. Out of the many Sahanas that the search has retrieved, only one of them has checked in half an hour ago. Do have a look at her." The librarian turned the monitor of his computer to face the others so that they could see her photo.

"Wonderful. It will reduce our work to a great extent. Thanks!" The Inspector turned towards Vishu and asked, "Can you see if she is in the main reading room? If not, then we might have to go up to the second level too."

"I am sorry. The second level is currently closed for maintenance. If she is not in the main reading room here, then you should be able to find her in the silent room adjacent to the café lounge over there," suggested the librarian pointing a finger in the direction of the café lounge.

Vishu craned his neck and walked a few steps into the main room. "I can't see Sahana here in the main room. We might find her inside the silent room. Sivu used to mention that they often met there. In fact, he also mentioned about a funny incident that happened in the silent room a few days ago."

The main room had a seating area at the center and the bookshelves all along the walls. The tables and chairs were aligned in a series of multiple aisles. He scanned each aisle from one end of it and then proceeded to the next. Ajay spoke for the first time since he entered the library. "Do you mind if I use your system to get some more information?" Without waiting for a reply, he entered the counter and the Librarian obliged by pulling a chair beside his. Vishu returned to the reception area where the Inspector and Akhila were waiting. The Inspector had become impatient, as the case seemed to stagnate. He was restlessly tapping his fingers on the counter. Akhila, on the other hand looked stern with a curled lip. She was slightly annoyed as she had been unable to talk to Vishu since the investigation had started and even during lunch he had dozed off at the Katte.

"Sir, Sahana is not here in the main room. She must be in the silent room for sure. Let's go there."

Ajay turned his chair away from the computer and said, "I have another suggestion. Let's all not go to the silent room. Akhila, why don't you go and get her here?" Akhila nodded and headed towards the silent room. Ajay turned towards Vishu and asked, "Could you tell us about the funny incident that happened with Sivu in the silent room?"

Vishu started laughing. "Apparently, Sivu and Sahana were stuck with a laptop which would not stop playing music. They were in the silent room when this happened. Though it was not intentional, they had to leave the place along with the faulty system."

The Inspector was confused. "How is this funny?"

"Sorry I wasn't very clear. Inside the 'Silent Room' we are not supposed to make any noise. See, students use the library to finish their assignments and have team discussions in the main reading room. But in the silent room, you are supposed to study all by yourself without disturbing others. Students end up whispering with one another if they need to discuss anything. The other day, while Sivu and Sahana were whispering in the silent room, Sahana's laptop started playing music loudly. They couldn't stop the music and they eventually had to run out of the library with the laptop. I feel bad for the students inside silent room on that day."

An accusatory voice came from the other side of the counter. "Do you really feel sorry for those students? From what I remember, you were amused that day and not even slightly remorseful. In fact, you guys ran away while I was still talking."

⊲∋◆∁⊳

Akhila crossed the café lounge and the long corridor to reach the entrance of the silent room. The two glass doors had the college logo and name on one of them, and the other had the sign 'For students only'. She had to use all her might to pull the door open, as it seemed to have a vacuum seal. The heavy door was a soundproof measure ensuring that the silent room remained so irrespective of external decibel levels. She entered the room and was welcomed by silence, a rare commodity within the college campus. She noticed that the tables and chairs were arranged in two distinct rows. Each table had a cubicle kind of enclosure, which despite being small, provided privacy for students while studying. The enclosures helped students pursue various activities – some did their assignments and studies, a few munched on snacks, others napped in between their study schedule and some others listened to music or watched movies. The enclosures made it difficult for Akhila to locate Sahana without peeking in at each and every table in order to see the faces of the people. She walked from one table to another and trying to remember Sahana's face from the computer screen that she saw a few minutes ago. Cursing herself for not taking a good second look at the photo, she proceeded further. She did remember that Sahana wore glasses and that she had short hair that fell to just above her shoulders. Frantically she peeped into all the tables on either side of the row. A few students didn't enjoy the intrusion and gave her a cold stare.

She was almost at the end of the aisle and there was still no sign of Sahana. At the far end of the aisle, a girl got up and left her desk. She wore glasses and she had her hair in a ponytail. Instantly, Akhila rushed towards her. By the time she reached the desk however, the other girl had entered the restroom. Akhila was left with no option but to wait beside her desk till the girl returned. The girl's laptop was open and the screen was locked. Her phone was plugged into the laptop for charging. There was a half-eaten packet of chips and a cola can next to it. A handbag hung on one of the arms of the chair and a jacket hung at the back of it. Akhila thought the girl would return soon but she was getting impatient now. As she stood there waiting, her thoughts wandered from one topic to another. How well did Sivu and Sahana get along? Why was Sivu attracted to a geeky girl who spent more time in the library than anywhere else? Was she even aware of the fact that Sivu had gone missing? She tried to block all these thoughts in vain.

A faint vibration disturbed her thoughts. For a moment, she could not figure out what the source of the noise was. She soon realized that it was a cell phone's vibration and pulled out her phone from her jacket to confirm that it was not her cell phone that was ringing. She looked on the table and saw Sahana's phone vibrating. But her attention was riveted on to something else on the phone. The wallpaper of the phone became visible as the phone rang and it was a photo of the girl and a guy with a familiar face. It was Vishu. She was shocked for a moment and rubbed her eyes in disbelief. However, before she opened her eyes, the phone stopped vibrating and the screen got locked again. It blacked out and she did not get a second chance to verify if it was actually Vishu in the photo. She was so tired and exhausted with the ongoing case. Throughout the whole fiasco, thoughts about Vishu were constantly running in the back of her mind. For the same reason, she dismissed the thought of seeing him on the wallpaper. She checked her watch and grumbled.

"Excuse me. This is my desk," came a low voice from behind.

"Are you Sahana?" Akhila asked.

"Yeah. Do I know you?"

"I am Akhila, Vishu's friend," she introduced herself. "Vishu is Sivu's close friend. Have you heard from Sivu lately? He has been missing for the past few days and everyone is worried. Vishu has registered a compliant with the Police and they are at the reception of the library doing their investigation as we speak."

Sahana looked shocked. "Oh my god. I have not heard from Sivu for the last four days. It has always been like that since I have known him. We meet up once or twice in a week. I didn't try contacting him thinking that he would be busy with his project. I never thought he would be in trouble. In fact, I had plans of meeting him this weekend."

"Vishu believes that he has been kidnapped. Srini and Avi are missing too."

"Oh my God. That's so terrible. I wish I had known about this before. What do we do now?" asked a teary-eyed Sahana.

"The Inspector, his team and Vishu are waiting outside. They might have a few questions for you. Please come along."

"Sure. I will come. Let me first clear my desk and pack my stuff." Sahana trashed the cola can and the chips packet in the nearby dustbin. She returned to the desk and unplugged her cell phone. She logged into her laptop to save her work before shutting down the system. Akhila could hear Sahana sobbing and she felt sorry for her. It was bad enough that Sivu had gone missing, but on top of that, she was not even aware of the news.

She removed the handbag from the chair and put her phone inside. While she wore her coat, she controlled her emotions and asked, "Do they have any leads so far? Are they suspecting anyone?"

Akhila did not respond. Sahana turned around to face Akhila who stood rooted to the spot. She had been staring at the laptop screen all this while. Sahana went near her and shook her shoulders. Akhila turned to her and broke down. "Hey, what happened to you? Why are you crying?" Sahana asked. Akhila did not reply and continued crying all the while staring at the laptop. Sahana could not understand what went wrong. She turned towards the desk and tried to figure out what had happened. She had only her laptop on the desk along with her handbag. The laptop screen was visible. The wallpaper was a photo of a couple smiling and sitting next to each other. The girl was bespectacled and had flowing short hair. The guy was lean and had a boyish smile. He sported spectacles with an unmistakable red frame. It wasn't Sahana and Sivu, but Sahana and Vishu in the photo. The Vishu that Akhila had come to love.

"Akhila, are you alright? Talk to me. What happened?" Akhila was upset and did not want to talk to her. She ran to the exit without a word and Sahana followed, grabbing her laptop in hand.

⟺⟐⟐⟐⟺

"Excuse me?" Vishu looked up to see who had made the comment. It was the librarian, Pradeep, throwing accusatory daggers at him. "What did you say? Remorseful? Why should I be remorseful?"

"If someone disturbs the students in the library especially by playing music in the silent room, I would expect them to be a bit remorseful at the least."

"Are you kidding me? I was telling Ajay about Sivu and Sahana playing loud music in the silent room and you are accusing me instead."

"I am just telling you the truth. You were the one who ran out with Sahana that day. I was still scolding you and you didn't even wait for me to finish."

"You are getting confused now. It was Sivu…" Before he could complete his sentence, the sound of people running distracted them. They saw Akhila running towards them from the silent room sobbing. Sahana followed her right behind. Vishu stopped Akhila and asked, "What happened? Is everything alright?"

Akhila gave Vishu a disgusted stare and the next moment she slapped him right across his cheek in front of everyone. The Inspector raised his voice and said, "Alright. Stop this nonsense. What is going on here?"

Sahana had arrived at the scene by then. She saw Vishu in the group and hugged him tightly. "Thank goodness. You are fine. I was told that you were kidnapped and I got so worried. Although, she did not tell me that they had found you guys."

Everyone was confused. The constable said aloud, "I am going crazy. What the hell is happening?"

Vishu took a couple of moments to get a grasp of his crazed surrounding. Sahana was still holding on to him tightly and he tried to free himself. He was embarrassed as he was slapped by Akhila a few moments ago and was now in the arms of another girl. He pulled away from Sahana, turned to a furious Akhila and said, "Look I can explain… Err I mean, I cannot explain… I don't know what is happening." He turned to Sahana and asked, "Who are you? Do I know you?"

Sahana was taken aback. She screamed, "What the hell? Are you really asking me who I am? After all these months of dating and going around town, you ask me if you know me? You try to explain this situation to this girl in front of me and ask me that who 'I' am? What is wrong with you Sivu?"

"Sivu? I am sorry! We have been looking for Sivu since the past two days. I am Vishu. You must be mistaken," remarked Vishu.

"I trusted you all this while Vishu. I am shocked that you did something disgusting like this. How could you even think of cheating? Sahana, we both have been cheated by the same guy." Akhila had stopped sobbing by then.

"What nonsense are you talking about Akhila? Are you out of your mind? Let's sit down and sort the confusion out," suggested Vishu.

Akhila snatched the laptop from Sahana's hands and showed the wallpaper photo on the laptop to Vishu. "Now, what do you have to say for yourself?"

Vishu stared at the photo in the laptop. The guy in the photo was himself with spectacles. The background in the photo was the library. He was sitting with the girl who had hugged him a couple of minutes ago. He was smiling and holding her in the photo. He got confused. "Could anyone tell me what is happening? I am in a photo that was taken inside the library along with this girl whom I have never met before. Is this some kind of trick?"

It was Ajay's turn to speak. He had been doing some research on the librarian's computer till now and he turned around to face everyone. "It is true that Vishu was here the other day with Sahana. I saw the check-in logs and the video of the day when they ran away from the library with Sahana's laptop."

The constable was confused. "So you mean this guy is two timing the girls? I never thought a guy like him could cheat."

"No. You do not understand. Vishu is not cheating anyone. In fact, he is not aware of Sahana yet," clarified Ajay.

"What rubbish? Sivu and I have been seeing each other for the last few months."

"Exactly. Sivu and you are seeing each other. Vishu and Akhila are dating too. But Sivu has been missing for the past three days. So are Avi and Srini."

"I am not sure how Srini and Avi are involved in this now?" questioned Akhila.

Ajay smiled and said calmly, "Oh they all have been in the picture always. Don't you get it? You see, Vishu, Sivu, Srini and Avi are all the same person."

CHAPTER 10

There was complete silence in the reception area. The onlookers had stopped murmuring among themselves and paid attention to the ongoing conversation.

"I am sorry? Seriously, what?" said a dumbstruck Vishu. He could not understand anything Ajay Kumar said.

"Why don't we all go to the café lounge and I will explain," suggested Ajay.

"Well, sounds good. Clear the crowd and cordon the lounge for us, will you?" the Inspector nodded while ordering the Constable who set to work instantly.

Ajay pulled his chair close to Vishu's in the lounge. He pulled out a notebook and pen to take some notes and said, "Before I say anything more, I would like you to answer a few of my questions."

Vishu was annoyed. "I am sorry. I need to be alone for some time." His mind was still reeling from seeing the photo with Sahana. He headed to the exit.

The Inspector stopped him midway. "Please come with us for just a few minutes. I will explain. Dr. Ajay Kumar is my friend and a Psychiatrist by profession. I wanted him to talk to you. It will not take long." Something about the Inspector's voice told him that he was not going to take a no for an answer and he agreed hesitantly.

Dr. Ajay asked, "Since when do you know your friends?"

"Since the first day of college. Nearly six months now."

"That's nice. How well do you know each of them?" He jotted down something. Vishu was not able to see what he scribbled.

"I know them very well. They are my close friends here. I hang out with them all the time."

"Can you tell me more about them?"

"Sure. Hmm. Sivu is a tall lean guy. He is the cool one in the group. He has excellent communication skills. He comes to college in a scooter. Then comes Avi. He …"

"Sorry to interrupt for a second. Inspector, can you hand me the case file?" He took the file and flipped over few pages. "You can continue Vishu."

"Avi is a jovial guy. He is very good at studies. He follows cricket religiously and listens to a lot of music. Srini is the one who takes all the decisions. We call him the boss of our group."

"You said Sivu rides a scooter, right?" Vishu nodded. "Sahana, have you seen Sivu with his scooter?"

"I haven't. Although he did talk about having one on a few occasions."

"Okay. Vishu, continue."

"They stay together in the hostel and we used to meet at Katte. We stayed in campus long after class hours talking every day."

"Why didn't you stay with them in the hostel?"

"I rented a room close to the campus before the classes had begun. The lease ends in a year. I cannot leave the room in the middle of the lease period."

"Tell me more about your friends."

"What else do you want to know? I already told you everything."

"I want to know about their background. Where they are from?"

"Sivu is from Shimoga. Avi is from Yellapur and Srini is from Bangalore."

"Cool!" Dr. Ajay jotted down few points in his notebook and gave a pause to his rapid round of questions. "Tell me about their families. What do they do? Do they have any siblings?"

"Families? I don't know about their families." Vishu was getting flustered and it was evident from the look on his face.

"You said you are close to your friends. Isn't it strange that you don't know about their families?"

"Why is it strange? We never talked about our families."

"Close friends talk to each other about everything. Families are something everyone talks about."

"I guess it just never came up."

"So you are saying that in the last six months there was not one occasion when any of you mentioned parents or brothers or sisters?"

Vishu was losing his patience "I do not understand why this is important. May I please leave now?" He turned to the Inspector and said "I am sorry I will not be able to accompany you today for further investigation. I hope you find my friends."

Dr. Ajay stared at Vishu for few seconds and then in a serious tone said, "Vishu, I am afraid he will not be able to find your friends. Actually, it is slightly complicated." After a pause he continued, "You suffer from Multiple Personality

Disorder (MPD). Basically, your friends live inside your head!"

Looking at the blank faces surrounding him, Dr. Ajay decided to continue, "Okay. Let me explain what multiple personality disorder is and how you tie into it." Dr. Ajay paused for a bit and it seemed as if he was gathering the appropriate words before uttering them. "It is a mental condition induced by a series of events that happens in one's life. In order to cope with the situations, a person with this disorder develops additional personalities."

Vishu listened to Dr. Ajay with his mouth wide open. His day was spiraling out of control with each passing moment. First his girlfriend doubted him and now his identity was being questioned. He had known MPD only in movies and books till now. He could not imagine himself being a victim. Everyone was waiting for an explanation of Vishu's current state. But Vishu just sat there staring at Dr. Ajay.

Dr. Ajay continued "Usually, these conditions are linked to an event which leaves a significant impact in one's mind. Such events leave a lasting impression and sometimes they manifest into a personality within you. Tell me, what do you think are the strongest points of each of your friends, something you like them for?"

"Hmm. Srini is good at making decisions for the group and he handles difficult situations well. Sivu has excellent communication skills. Avi is a music lover and fond of poetry."

"Do you think you can do any of these? Do you think you have any of these strengths? Do you speak confidently?" Dr. Ajay carried on.

"No. I get nervous around people," Vishu said timidly.

"If I have to guess, you find it hard to make decisions. And chances are that you don't have an interest in fine arts like music. Am I right?" Vishu nodded in agreement. "You reveled in their company and did not indulge in having other friends."

"Are you saying that I used to become one of them and behave like them?"

"Your personality changed in different situations. The stronger person then would come out."

"Then how come I was able to see them too?"

"There are varying side effects with MPD. Some conditions have special characteristics. Some of the MPD patients even suffer from hallucination. They see things and hear voices of imaginary people. In your case, you were able to see the other three personalities while behaving like them at times."

Akhila was listening to this conversation dumbfounded. She could not believe that the guy she liked was living in a world that he had created. She began thinking about how could nobody had noticed any of this before when it suddenly struck her. "On the first day of college, he introduced himself as four different people when the seniors were ragging him. I always thought he was just trying to trick the seniors."

"I guess this is why the senior responded weirdly when you all met him earlier." Vishu was taken by surprise. Before he could ask anything, Dr. Ajay said, "I also heard about what the security guard at the stadium had to say."

"Raju had seen all of us together. How can you explain that?" Vishu was fighting back his tears. A huge part of him still refused to believe that anything could be wrong with him.

Dr. Ajay stood up from his chair and walked around Vishu. "We went to meet the security guard, Raju, at the stadium. Apparently, he suffers from double visions when he is drunk. The other day, he was not sure if he saw four guys on the way to terrace. But in front of the Inspector, he accepted immediately the moment the topic about his borrowing money came up. I believe he might have seen blurred images of you on that day and not your imaginary friends."

"I spent an entire semester with them. How can all of that happen inside my head? We hung out together all the time. We went to classes together. How can all of that be imaginary?" Vishu eyes were welling up with tears now.

"Vishu, the sooner you accept the truth, the better it is for you. We are trying to help you. Please understand. The admission office does not have any records of Srini, Avi or Sivu. Your professors do not recall any such students in the class. None of them have been able to confirm if you had friends or not. We spoke to Professor Ravi Nagraj. He mentioned that you sat alone most of the time in a bench that can seat four students."

Vishu tried to protest, but the words seemed to be stuck in his throat. "Let's look at the other things. The dog, what's his name, Muffin. Dogs do not go play with random people unless they know them well enough. You played with the dog as Avi and not as anyone else. The dog responded to you in the same way as any other day when you saw it outside the cafeteria today. It does not know if it was your other personality who played with it. It only knows your face and touch and responds to you."

Vishu was left speechless. He continued listening with a nonchalant face. "Anyone who knows you has seen only you.

They have not seen any of your friends. We spoke to the lab instructor, Mrs. Jayashree Nath. She was able to confirm our suspicion. You had told us that the four of you were in the same batch. She showed us the record of the exam and you were the only person in the viva the other day."

He tried to grasp all the information he had just heard without reacting. He stopped crying as he began to realize the gravity of the situation.

"Now, let's look at your friends. Let's start with Sivu! Sahana and the librarian have known your alter personality - Sivu. Without your knowledge, your alter personality took complete control of you every time you met Sahana. You even wore a red-framed spectacle when you became Sivu. The same was found later at the terrace of the stadium, remember? The frame has your fingerprints on it. We got the reports from the lab."

"I stopped by your room earlier today to get your fingerprints for ID purposes. We had no option left," the Inspector said.

Dr. Ajay continued, "We spoke to some people who work at the cafeteria about you. They mentioned that you always placed an order for four. Even at the coffee kiosk, you ordered four cups of coffee and left three behind. Please try to look at all the evidences and understand the situation. The sooner you come to terms with it, the faster we can start working on it."

Everyone was listening intently. No one said anything. Vishu was in his complete senses now. He began to grasp the reality of the situation, the one that suggested he was indeed suffering from a serious medical condition. All the memories of his friendship and the time he had spent with Srini, Avi and Sivu seemed artificial. He broke down again.

The Inspector tried to console him, but Dr. Ajay silently motioned him not to. Vishu just put his head down on the table and started sobbing. After a few minutes, Vishu tried to pull himself together and looked up. He wiped his tears away and sat upright. He turned to the Inspector and said "Thank you, Sir. For helping me through this."

"You are welcome. Remember, I had promised I would find out the truth about your friends. Now don't worry, we will get you out of this as well."

Vishu smiled at him. "How were you able to find out? When did you think of involving the Doctor?"

"To be honest, I just ran out of leads. I was getting little worried because nothing was falling in place. I did not smell anything fishy until this afternoon during lunch. I went through the FIR again and something caught my attention. By the way, I wanted to ask if Sivu had an initial in his name – 'W'?"

"Yes. Siva W Sharan," Vishu nodded with confirmation.

"Hah! I knew it. I was right!" the Inspector punched his fist with fervor.

"Why is it so important?"

"Vishu, I saw something unusual in the report given by you. Without your knowledge, you had left a clue for us to crack the case."

"What clue did I leave? I don't understand how I could have left a clue without realizing it."

"Let me explain. What were the full names of your friends?"

"Srinavas Wah"

"Siva Sharan W"

"Avinash Swar"

"Interestingly, all the three names have the same number of letters and the same alphabet set." The Inspector continued, "Another surprising thing is that all these names are anagrams of another name and that is none other than your name –

"Vishwas Rana"

Everyone in the lounge gasped at what the Inspector said. They took few seconds to digest the information. Vishu could not believe his ears. He wondered how he had used his name to arrive at three other names without his knowledge.

"Subconsciously, you have come up with the other three names using your own name. Hence, you don't have any clue about it," assured Dr. Ajay.

There was silence in the room. Everyone present around Vishu was cautious of not hurting him any further. Akhila asked softly "What shall we do next? We can take back the case now. It is no longer a kidnapping, at least not one we know of."

"Leave it to me. I will take care of the case. Vishu, don't you worry. Dr. Ajay will take good care of you. You will be cured completely. Isn't it Dr. Ajay?" the Inspector turned to Dr. Ajay for some support to boost Vishu's spirits.

"Of course. In a matter of few months and under my observation, definitely he will be cured."

"Few months? But what about my studies and college?"

"I will talk to the Principal and get permission for you to be away for a few months on a sabbatical. You can always resume your studies once you are hale and healthy."

"In that case, I will go ahead and make arrangements for his admission at the hospital. That way, I can start my treatment immediately." Dr. Ajay got ready to leave the place.

"Perfect! Let's do it then…"

"Do I really have to be in a hospital? Can't I stay in my room and attend classes while taking some medicines?" Vishu got cold feet on hearing that an admission to the hospital was required for a few months.

"Medicines can get you only so far. The kind of treatment that you will be receiving will be a combination of medicines, seminars and therapy sessions. We will be running a series of tests after which we can chalk out a program for your specific condition." Dr. Ajay replied.

The Inspector added in, "Also, you will be undergoing treatment at one of the best hospitals in India – Neuro Science Hospital (NSH). Dr. Ajay is the head of the psychiatric wing. Trust me, you will be in good hands."

Vishu reluctantly agreed to the offer. Actually, he did not have any choice. A part of him wanted to run out of the room and hide somewhere. However, a part of him wanted to be cured and he stayed on.

"You take some time to get ready to leave for the hospital. Pack your belongings and be ready. I will personally come and pick you up. Meanwhile, let me go close the case." The Inspector thanked the librarian for his timely help and walked out of the library.

"I will see you soon at the hospital. Bye for now." Dr. Ajay waved his hand and followed the Inspector.

Sahana and Akhila were the two people left now at the café lounge along with Vishu. They were speechless at the turn of activities that had occurred in the last few minutes. Vishu was in no position to talk to them. He looked at them; both were crying and he felt a sharp pain in his chest. He knew that he had caused a lot of pain to both Sahana and Akhila and yet he knew that he would never have done something like that knowingly. He looked into their eyes, gave them an apologetic wave of hand and headed out of the room. Not until he was out of their sight did he let the sobs rip out of his chest.

⋙◆⋘

Neuro Science Hospital - NSH, spread across 150 acres, was situated in the southern part of Bangalore city. The campus was a lush green arena, a different world from the concrete jungle outside the walls. The main entrance that led to the road had buildings on either side. Each building housed one or more specialized wings. It was noted for its Psychiatry department that included Child Psychiatry, De-addiction services, Obsessive compulsive disorder, Dissociative Identity disorder to name a few. The Inspector picked Vishu up as promised and dropped him at the hospital. Vishu had packed all his belongings from the room in which he stayed and vacated the place. He informed his parents and they needed a couple of days to reach Bangalore, as they currently stayed in a small city in northern India.

Vishu entered the campus through the main entrance and headed directly towards the Psychiatry block. The Inspector ensured that the admission procedure was completed smoothly. After the Inspector bid good-bye to Vishu, he was taken to a ward on the second floor of the block. He was taken to his room. His world had been condensed to a sterile steel bed with white sheets and a side table with some magazines stacked on it. He met his roommate, a short guy who looked at him with expressionless eyes. He was dressed in a green gown, which was the hospital norm. Vishu took a deep sigh as he set his things on the bed. Once he finished an early dinner that was served to him by one of the nurses, he was curious to know when he could meet Dr. Ajay. So he struck up a conversation with the nurse who was administering an injection to him.

"Ah that hurts. Why are you giving me an injection?"

"This is part of the initial prescription. It will put you to sleep."

"Okay. What's your name? And when can I meet Dr. Ajay Kumar? He said he would take good care of me."

"I am Stella Mary", the nurse replied. She disposed the syringe in the safe sharps disposal container. "He comes in every other day. Tomorrow is going to be a busy day for you with various tests scheduled in the morning. I hope you…"

Vishu was no longer listening. He was lying curled up on his side. The nurse covered him with a blanket and said in a low voice "I hope you are ready!" She left the ward.

CHAPTER 11

Vishu woke up to the sound of a loud commotion going on around his bed. He soon realized that he was not in his ward anymore. His bed was being wheeled away by the hospital staff. Two men held the bed on either ends and maneuvered it while a nurse, with whom Vishu had interacted last night, was walking along side with few files in hand. It looked like they were in a hurry to take him somewhere. The nurse said something to the other two and they nodded their heads in agreement.

"Hey! Nurse Stella, right? Where are you taking me?"

"You are awake. Good! We will be conducting few tests on you as I mentioned yesterday night," answered Nurse Stella.

"So early? The sun hasn't even risen yet." Vishu had glanced at one of the open windows and saw that it was still dark out there.

"Yes, the tests are usually done early in the morning while fasting, you know, on an empty stomach."

"What tests are these? How long will they take?"

"The Doctor will brief you in a while. Now just lie down, will you?" The disgruntled nurse silenced Vishu.

While the nurses wheeled the bed to the Diagnostic Laboratory Center, Vishu gazed at the passing tube lights in the ceiling and kept quiet. He quickly realized that he was alone and had no one to hold his hand through this. There was nobody by his side to give him the much-needed moral support during this phase. He had left everything in the hands of the Dr. Ajay, who had promised to cure him soon. But he was anxious too as he had not seen Dr. Ajay since the day he arrived at the hospital. One glimpse of the Doctor would have reduced his anxiety to a great extent. As they entered the Diagnostic Laboratory Center, Vishu noticed that it was well insulated with two sets of heavy doors, which closed with a *hsssh* sound. This ensured that the place was very clean with no signs of dust or any other form of contaminants. The Laboratory was a big room with numerous sophisticated machines. He couldn't identify what they were used for or what they did. There were separate rooms at the end of Laboratory and on one of the doors was a sign that read 'Consultation'. Vishu presumed that within the rooms, the patients were prescribed medication based on the reports obtained from the tests carried out in the Laboratory.

Vishu was taken to one of the chairs that he assumed were meant for observing the patients. The nurse helped him get off the bed and made him sit on the chair. Once seated, he looked up to see some kind of headgear being fitted to the chair. To his left, he saw a console with multiple displays. A customized keyboard was present below the displays. He deduced that all the controls for the devices around the chair on which he was sitting were housed in that equipment and one or more displays were hooked to the devices around him. The nurse plugged in some of the cables from the equipment to Vishu's chest and the display started to show a graph and beep at regular intervals. He was staring at the displays trying to understand what it showed. Vishu heard footsteps and he hoped to see Dr. Ajay. However, the Doctor who entered was someone else to his surprise. The Doctor greeted everyone with a methodical nod and headed to the equipment straightaway. He looked at some of the displays and noted something in the notebook on the table. He began instructing the nurse to set up things for tests in the adjacent room. After the nurse left, he went back to the equipment and began pressing some buttons. He approached Vishu and felt his pulse, his eyes on the machine all the while. Vishu was getting restless as no one was explaining what was happening to him.

"Doctor!" He interrupted and asked, "Where is Dr. Ajay Kumar? I have not seen him since yesterday."

"Dr. Ajay does not come here every day. He is the head of the department and he has many other duties," replied the Doctor without even looking at him. He pulled out a small phial from one of the cabinets along with a syringe. He squeezed out the liquid into the syringe and rubbed Vishu's shoulder to loosen his muscles. "Hold still for a second!" He said as he pricked the needle into his arm. Vishu clenched his teeth. He asked, "What medicine was that? And what are these tests for?"

The Doctor realized that Vishu was afraid and he explained the tests that were going to be conducted on Vishu. "Don't be nervous. These are normal procedures. You have been plugged to a multi parameter monitor, which is capable of monitoring the current state of a patient. The displays you are seeing over here; each one has significance to it. The graph that you are seeing is the ECG – Electro Cardio graph: In simple words, the graph depicts the activity of your heart. You can see your pulse rate right next to the graph. The console below that is displaying your blood pressure. The one beside it is monitoring your respiration rate. The last one is current body temperature."

While Vishu was grasping each of the medical terms and continued to gape at the displays, the Doctor continued, "The injection I administered just now is for the MRI scanning which will be done next. This injection is a contrast dye and helps in getting better images of your brain. Once the nurse is back from the MRI scanning room, we will shift you over there and get your brain MRI done. The MRI will help Dr. Ajay to identify if there is any damage to brain tissue or vessels, internal bleeding or blood clots in the head. This test will give us an insight of your brain. Based on the reports, he will be in a better position to plan therapy for you."

The nurse returned and immediately Vishu was shifted to the adjacent room, which housed only one instrument. It had a single big circular tube. There was a bed that seemed to be halfway in the big tube. One of the walls of the room was fully made of glass. On the other side of the glass was a console of buttons and switches, which Vishu assumed, was present to control this circular instrument. He was asked to lie down on the bed with his neck nestled in a grove to hold his head still. The nurse quickly strapped his arms and legs to the bed. The Doctor entered the room and came close to Vishu and said, "This is the MRI scanning instrument. You will be moved a little further inside the circular opening at the center of the instrument. Try to stay still for at least ten minutes. Remember, no movements at all!"

The Doctor walked to the room behind the glass wall to turn on the instrument. He punched a few buttons on the console and the bed started to move further into the circular opening. Once Vishu's head was inside the circular opening, the bed stopped. The ceiling of the opening was so close to Vishu's face that he started feeling claustrophobic. He immediately wanted to get up but was unable to do so as he was strapped to the bed. He thought he would die out of suffocation inside that instrument. Fear was threatening to suffocate him and he was unable to even scream. He managed to close his eyes as tightly as possible. At that very moment, the instrument started to make a loud noise. He didn't dare open his eyes and forced himself to think of something pleasant that could calm him down. He imagined lying on a beach under a clear night sky and he started to count stars. This helped him relax and for a moment, he forgot about the MRI. After ten minutes, the instrument stopped making the noise and the bed started to move out. He slowly opened his eyes after the nurse unstrapped him from the bed.

Vishu got up and turned to face the Doctor who was entering the room. While the Doctor removed his gloves, he said to Vishu, "Dr. Ajay will be taking your psychotherapy sessions starting next week. Once he gets all the reports of these tests, he should be able to plan your medication. Do you have any questions?"

Vishu just nodded. The Doctor left the room after giving some instructions to the nurse. After a while, he was shifted to his bed. He felt very drowsy and he realized that it must be the effect of the medication. He was soon asleep. He woke up in the evening to the sound of a bird chirping. As it was getting dark, he switched on the light next to his bed. The same pair of expressionless eyes stared back at him without blinking. He thought of striking a conversation with his roommate and waved his hand. Even after introducing himself, his roommate did not respond. The grim face never made any welcoming gesture.

"He has been silent for many months now. He won't talk to anyone or respond to anything," said Nurse Stella, who had entered the room a couple of seconds before and saw Vishu trying to talk to the other patient.

"What happened to him?" asked Vishu.

"His also has Disassociate Identity Disorder."

"Is he cured now?"

"He has had more than a year of therapies and medications. We believe he is doing all right and showing positive results. He is being kept under observation as he has a history of sudden bursts of violence." Vishu started to sweat after knowing his roommate's story. Sensing his discomfort, the nurse said, "Don't worry. He is not a threat anymore. He would have been kept in isolation if he were a threat."

"I hope so. That is comforting. Thanks." Vishu smiled at the nurse and added slyly, "What is the procedure to change the room here?"

Nurse Stella chuckled as she kept the food tray on the table beside his bed and said, "Finish your dinner before it gets cold. I have kept your medicines beside the tray. Take them after you eat. Hit the buzzer next to the light switch if you need anything." With that, she left the room. Vishu took the food tray and placed it on his bed. It contained a simple diet: two rotis made of wheat, a curry, a cup of dal, rice and an apple. He remembered the tasty hot food served at his college campus and wondered if he would ever be able to taste it again. Sighing, he started eating the food and realized it was not as bad as he imagined it would be.

He soon finished the food and gulped down the pills with water. He kept the tray aside and turned off the light. Lying on the bed, he stared at the night sky through the window until he fell asleep again.

⊷❍◆❑⊷

"Relax. Let go of any thoughts in the mind. Close your eyes. How do you feel now?"

"Ahhh… It hurts!" Vishu screamed with pain as Dr. Ajay Kumar gave an injection to him once he closed his eyes.

"It's over. Don't open your eyes. Clear your mind and try to relax. Take deep breaths," said Dr. Ajay while removing the syringe and rubbing Vishu's hand with a piece of cotton. The therapy room was dimly lit and a soft, soothing music was playing in the background. Vishu was comfortably slouched in the reclining chair. Dr. Ajay sat in front of him in a revolving chair and had a small moveable desk beside him. Apart from his routine medical equipment, a note pad and pen were present to take down notes as and when needed. As advised by Dr. Ajay, Vishu was breathing slowing and deeply through his nose. The oxygen that reached his brain made him feel more relaxed. In a calm and relaxing voice, Dr. Ajay began to speak to him, "Now, you will fall asleep. Once you fall asleep, I would be able to talk to your subconscious and get to know you well. You have to cooperate with me throughout."

Vishu listened to Dr. Ajay and he nodded in agreement. He continued in the same tone, "I will be counting backwards from 100 to 0 slowly and you will get sleepier as time progresses. By the time I reach 0, you will be fast asleep."

100… *tap*… 99… *tap*… 98… *tap*… Dr. Ajay started counting as he tapped his foot with every count. Every 10 counts, he paused and said, "You are getting tired… You are falling asleep. By next 10 counts, you will be more tired."

52… *tap*… 51… *tap*… 50… "You are getting tired! You are feeling lighter and lighter!"

After around ten minutes, 2… *tap*… 1… *tap*… 0. By the time the he reached 0, Vishu was fast asleep. To ensure that Vishu's subconscious was responding to him, he asked Vishu to slowly touch the tip of his nose with his right hand. Vishu promptly obliged and touched his nose with his hand. Dr. Ajay continued talking to Vishu, "Imagine the DCE campus, the big gate, many buildings, garden at the entrance and the parking lot. Do you see all these Vishu?"

Vishu promptly replied, "Yes, I do."

"Now, I want you to imagine students all around the campus. Some are walking with their backpacks, few are sitting on the stone benches and few are in the cafeteria eating."

"Okay"

"Do you see your friends?" Dr. Ajay wanted to get an idea of what Vishu was actually seeing.

"Yes, I see them. Srini and Sivu are sitting on the stone bench and chatting. Avi is playing with muffin."

"Good. Let's talk about Avi. Tell me more about him – his nature, his likes and dislikes, hobbies, things like that." Dr. Ajay started scribbling down points as Vishu started to speak. After a few minutes of talking to Vishu's subconscious mind, Dr. Ajay was able to get few answers about Avi's personality and the reason for his existence within Vishu. A little bit of more prodding and he was able to speak directly to Vishu's alter personality, Avi.

"I have appeared at this hour and time,

For once, let me be more than just a mime;

Doctor, why don't you get off the dime,

And make use of this occasion, which is sublime."

"Wow. That's a fine poem. I am impressed. Avinash, right?"

"Thanks. I prefer Avi." He started to hum some song and snapped his fingers creating a tune for the song. Dr. Ajay was surprised at the qualities and mannerism of the personality within Vishu, which was unlike him.

"I have some questions for you, Avi. Will you be able to answer them?"

"Sure." Avi stopped humming and was all ears to what the Doctor had to ask.

"Since when do you know Vishu and how?"

"It goes back a long way. I think it was in high school. Vishu was in a classroom, an English lesson, with about a hundred students. The teacher was picking students randomly to come up to the front of the class and recite a poem. When it was Vishu's turn, he panicked and could not remember the poem. Even after someone handed him a book, he was so nervous that he began stammering. Everyone in the class laughed at him. He was babbling as he read the book. Some of the students began to mock him by babbling from the last benches. The teacher, instead of encouraging him, reprimanded him in front of other students. Vishu felt humiliated and angry at the same time for his incompetency. He wanted to prove that he could read and speak well in front of everyone. His lack of confidence deterred him from proving them wrong. He threw the book, turned around and ran away from the class. Wiping his tears with his hands, he went to an isolated place on the terrace of the school building. He cried for some time and started thinking about how he could read and speak well in front of everyone. After a while he got tired of sitting in the hot sun and dozed off. That's where I come in. In the evening, I woke him up and tried consoling him. I introduced myself as his new friend and I listened to his entire story. After hearing him out, I convinced that I would help him in future if a similar situation arose. I promised him that he wouldn't have to worry about poems and music as I am well versed in it," explained Avi.

"Vishu told me earlier that met you on the first day of engineering. Why would he say that if you met him in school?" Dr. Ajay looked at his notes and realized that Vishu's account of the story was different from what Avi had said.

Avi smiled, "We all agreed to start afresh as his friends at Engineering College from day one. We convinced him to believe the same. Vishu listens to us and agrees to everything we say."

"I have appeared at this hour and time,

For once, let me be more than just a mime;

Doctor, why don't you get off the dime,

And make use of this occasion, which is sublime."

Avi continued to hum the poem and was soon lost in his own thoughts. Dr. Ajay observed a few critical aspects of Vishu's mental health while conversing with Avi. He understood that even though Vishu was the host personality among the other personalities, he was the weakest of them all. The other personalities had the capacity to switch whenever Vishu was in a perceived psychosocial threat. He also noted that the other three personalities were aware of each other's coexistence and even interacted without Vishu's knowledge. Vishu also perceived that these other personalities were actually for real. He noted these points in his book and left the room, hoping that the next set of sessions would prove to be more helpful in getting to a diagnosis.

⊷ ⊃●⊂ ⊷

"Namma devara sathya namage gotthu!" replied Sivu when Dr. Ajay suggested that Vishu might not have been so low on confidence before the formation of other personalities. He was confused, "I am sorry. Is that Kannada? What does that mean?"

"It just means only we know him inside and out. What I really mean is that I disagree! Vishu was no good before we came into his life."

Dr. Ajay scribbled more notes. Sivu continued to talk, "It is nice weather out today, isn't it? Do you like this weather Doctor?"

"Not much. What about you?" Dr. Ajay asked the question without lifting his head.

"I like this weather a lot. It would be so nice to have a cup of coffee now."

"I can get you one after this session." Dr. Ajay buzzed the nurse and order one coffee for later.

"That's wonderful. Thank you. I have to say that I am pleasantly surprised with this hospital. It is well maintained and the staff is very well mannered. You guys are doing a great job!"

Dr. Ajay seemed surprised to see Sivu speak in a relaxed manner. His mannerisms and diction seemed very different and polished compared to Avi and Vishu. He asked, "Sivu, I need to ask you a question." Without waiting for an answer he added, "How did you meet Vishu? Can you describe meeting him?"

"I met Vishu in pre-university. It was a warm afternoon and classes had just ended for the day. When the students were leaving the classroom, Vishu found himself in front of some girls who were waiting in the corridor. I guess they were waiting there to bully someone and Vishu was their victim that day. They began flirting with him. Vishu, being the shy person that he is, began blushing. As they intensified their flirtatious questions, he began to stammer and sweat. That is when some of their friends joined in and began making fun of Vishu. He stood there listening to all their comments, just silently hanging his head. He didn't know what to say or do and left the place quietly. He narrated the incident to Avi who tried to console him and promised to find a solution to his speaking skills. The very next day, I came in and comforted Vishu."

"How was that a solution? How did that help Vishu?" Dr Ajay asked him.

"It did. I help him handle such situations. Vishu is confident in front of girls now. I don't think you have met Sahana, do you?"

"Sahana liked you, not him. You will be handling the situation as Sivu and not as Vishu. So, how are you helping him? It is certainly not helping him improve his weaknesses."

The conversation got Sivu thinking. He did not know how to respond to Dr. Ajay's question. They spoke for the next hour. By then, Dr. Ajay's notebook had two more pages of notes. He let Sivu rest in the therapy room for some time before he was shifted back to his room and advised the nurse regarding the next set of medications to be administered.

Dr. Ajay made a mental note to himself to ask some specific questions when he interviewed Vishu next. He was hoping that the next couple of sessions would help him get a hold on the entire state of Vishu's mental health.

⊷⊃◆⊂⊶

"So tell me! How did you meet Vishu?" Dr. Ajay continued the drill with Srini.

"Not too sure about the date. I met Avi and Sivu at the same time as well," replied Srini.

"Can you tell me how you met them? Was it a sticky situation?" Dr. Ajay was getting a faint idea of how the personalities formed after the previous sessions.

"Not really. I met them in a park one day."

Dr. Ajay looked surprised as he was hoping to see a different weakness in Vishu's character that Srini assumed he could solve. Srini's answer intrigued him further. He asked, "Avi is good at poetry, Sivu is good at talking to people. Vishu's is not good with both and they help him in that regard. Do you help Vishu in any special way?"

Srini said, "Not in any special way. Vishu lacks confidence and is indecisive on many occasions, unable to judge what is right for him. That makes it easy for others to take him for granted and use him. I make sure that does not happen. I take control of things when everything goes overboard. With Avi and Sivu around, chances are that it might happen more often than not."

Dr. Ajay looked at his notes, "They all call you the boss. Correct?"

Srini shrugged the comment away and said "Ha. It is just for fun though I do take care of them all the time."

"So, I assume you take more responsibilities than the others. Let me ask you a question, the same one I asked Sivu earlier when I met him. Do you really think you folks are helping Vishu? The only reason he is in the hospital right now instead of attending college is because of you and the others."

Srini was taken aback. Dr. Ajay's remark made him think. He asked, "How can you say that Doctor? With our help, Vishu can do things that he can't even imagine doing alone. Without Avi, he cannot be good at poetry and music. Without Sivu, he would not have had the guts to ask Akhila out. I am sure I have helped him get out of tricky spots many a times in the past."

"Think about this. Has Vishu gotten any better in all those aspects when you guys are not around? Do you know when he heard about his condition in the library, he was not able to speak for hours? Do you seriously expect that you guys will be around him all the time to assist him in doing things? He needs to develop his personality on his own accord. He needs more space and freedom. Srini, try to understand the situation and Vishu's mental health. You guys comfort him but do not contribute to his well-being. In fact, he has become weaker and more helpless."

Dr. Ajay continued after a pause, "Srini, you need to let Vishu take control of situations more often. He needs to handle them and learn from them. You and the others should not have to help him overcome situations all the time. Do you understand what I am saying?"

Srini was busy recollecting the episodes from the past and did not reply. He remembered how Vishu was humiliated in the classroom when the Professor had asked him a question. They did not help him that time and instead had chosen to comfort him in the parking lot later. In another episode, Vishu was caught moving the desk from one classroom to another during a test and he was nervous and fumbled for words in front of the Supervisor. Once again, Srini and the others had spoken to him only later in the evening. Dr. Ajay's theory made sense to Srini. It seemed strange to him that all this while their existence was the problem.

Dr. Ajay interjected again and asked, "Srini, do you understand what I am saying?"

Srini replied teary eyed, "I do. I never thought that we were just hiding the real problem in Vishu instead of helping him get rid of it. Doctor, tell me how can I help him?"

Dr. Ajay smiled, "Thanks. I knew I could count on you. Now, let me summarize Vishu's mental state. There are four personalities within Vishu: You, Sivu, Avi and Vishu himself – who is the host personality. You three should come together to aid Vishu. Currently, if Vishu is in a situation, the host personality is switched with a more capable personality thereby making Vishu incompetent. We need to find a more adaptive coping strategy for Vishu than switching when in distress."

"Adaptive strategy? What does that mean?"

"After I spoke to all the personalities, I noticed each one of you bear a specific quality which Vishu could make use of. You should focus on supporting Vishu with these qualities instead of switching the personalities. To quote a well-known Psychiatrist here, 'Fusion of personalities' states is the key while retaining of experiences possessed in all of them'. The end goal of this exercise should be to integrate all the qualities more adaptively into the overall host personality structure. Do you understand what needs to be done?" Srini nodded in agreement.

"Will you be talking to the other personalities and help everybody come to a logical conclusion? All I ask from you three folks is unity and support."

"Yes," said Srini affirmatively. Dr. Ajay gave him instructions on how to approach the other personalities and guide them to support Vishu in the required way. At the end of the session, Dr. Ajay left the room and heaved a sigh of relief. He was hopeful that this session would bring out the results he had intended. Srini seemed to understand what had to be done.

CHAPTER 12

A few months into therapy, Vishu started showing significant improvements in his mental condition. The medicines were taking full effect as therapy sessions were reduced to every fortnight. Srini, Avi and Sivu were rarely seen during the therapy sessions unless Vishu was heavily sedated. There were no incidents during the regular times. They were slowly fizzling out from Vishu's mind though he was exhibiting their qualities once in a while.

"How are you feeling now Vishu? You are showing great results."

"Never been better I would say, Doctor," replied Vishu confidently.

"If you exhibit the same behavior for a month, I assure you that I will declare you fit and you can get out of here. Just hang in there and stick to the regime for some more time."

"Thanks. I am looking forward to that day," smiled Vishu.

"Sure. That day isn't far off. All you need to do is build your confidence level up. You don't need other personalities to help you in times of crisis. You can handle the situation well by yourself. Forget the incidents from the past. Talk to people, strike up friendships and be social. Your confidence level will automatically increase. Share your thoughts and communicate. Don't worry about whether they are going to laugh at it."

Dr. Ajay realized that Vishu wanted to leave the hospital early, which motivated him to take therapy seriously. He wished Vishu luck, patted him on the back and left the room. Vishu had indeed come a long way. His recovery was speedy and Dr. Ajay was delighted with the results.

⊷⫍⬥⫎⊶

After six months of therapy at the hospital, Vishu was declared fit and was allowed to leave the hospital premises. To ensure that memories of the past would not haunt him again during his studies Dr. Ajay had transferred him to another college in the city. The Inspector Aditya Shetty personally came to drop him to the college entrance. Vishu got down from the jeep and pulled his luggage out from the back.

"You take care of yourself Vishu. Call me if you need anything."

"Definitely Sir. I will do that." They both exchanged good byes and Vishu stood there till the jeep went out of his sight.

Vishu turned around and on the other side of the road was the entrance of the college. A huge board with blue font across a white background read "Regional College of Engineering" both in English and Kannada. The board spanned the entire width of the two gates meant for people to enter and exit respectively. There was a security office in between the gates with two guards inside monitoring screens while one was at the gate. Vishu noticed big trees from a distance, as the compound of the campus was not high enough. Among them were loads of Coconut and Ashoka trees. Regional College of Engineering was one of the oldest colleges, other than DCE, in the city established in early 1960s. The college was located in the outskirts of the city and was spread across a few acres of land. It had a reputation of bringing out the very best in students at the end of four years of college. Vishu crossed the road and began walking towards the main gate tugging his luggage. He came to a halt at the gate and wondered for a moment how this journey was going to be. He quickly bounced back from the trance and approached the security guard, who was sitting just outside the gate. He inquired about the directions to the hostel and the guard pointed him in the right direction. As he walked further inside the campus, he noticed a huge field to his left. A few students were playing cricket despite the hot sun and a lone Peepal tree in the field came to their rescue by providing shade to some part of the field. Admissions office and cafeteria were right across the field. Once he went past the field, the various departments and the classrooms were housed on either side of the pathway. It was a long walk from the entrance of the college and by the time he reached the hostel block, he was tired of dragging his luggage. He was allotted a room in the 'C' block. He saw a group of guys chatting in front of the hostel entrance. He went up to them and asked, "Excuse me. Do you guys know where the C block is?"

"No idea dude. We are new to the campus too." A tall lean guy from the group showed his bag while replying to Vishu.

"Oh cool. I am Vishwas Rana and I will be joining the Computer Science department."

"I am Vikram and I am going to pursue Mechanical engineering," the tall guy introduced himself and shook hands. The rest followed the same.

"I am Srinath. I am joining Mechanical too." said the second guy standing beside Vikram.

"I'm Avneesh. Mechanical department," said the guy next to Srini.

"It may seem strange but let me guess. Are you Sivu?" quipped Vishu facing the fourth guy.

"Weird. I am Sivaram. Some of my friends call me Sivu." Everyone was surprised except Vishu.

Vishu was puzzled. He pinched himself to make sure it was real. When it hurt, he stopped and turned to the tall guy and said, "You see these guys too, right?" He pointed to others.

Vikram gave him a suspicious look. "What's wrong with you? Of course, I can see these guys." Little did he realize the amount of relief that his affirmation bought Vishu.

"Thanks. It's a long story. I will explain some other time."

"Hey! What's happening here? What are you both talking about pointing at us?" questioned Srinath.

"He thought he was dreaming up people. I think he is still in vacation mode and he is acting just a little bit weird," remarked Vikram with a smile.

Vishu smiled and said, "Sorry about that. I promise I will explain later. Let's go find our rooms first."

They all nodded and headed towards the hostel. They carried their luggage and walked towards the security guard at the entrance of the hostel. The guard was sitting on a plastic chair with a stick resting on the arm of the chair. He stood up as these guys went near him.

Vikram asked the guard, "Do you know where Blocks 'B' and 'C' are?" He turned around to Vishu to confirm if his block was C and the rest were allotted rooms in block B.

The security guard just stared without reacting. Vikram turned to Vishu and said, "Looks like he doesn't understand English. Do any of you know Kannada?" Vishu came forward and questioned the guard in Kannada. The guard replied with directions on how to reach their respective blocks. He did not stop at that and queried about the computer facility and the Internet options available at the hostel. He got a simple answer that the guard was not aware of those things. The guys around Vishu started laughing at him. They were amused to see Vishu asking about Internet options to a security guard.

"What's wrong with that? I just wanted to know the details," argued Vishu.

"Isn't it too early to be looking for lab? And moreover, you are asking the wrong person. I guess all you folks in Computer Science are nerds. You are one even before you start your course," joked Vikram.

"Don't call me a nerd. I am not one."

"You are a geek then. You look like one too!" Avneesh made the comment as he entered the building. The others followed him leaving Vishu behind.

"Way to go Vishu. What a first impression you made!" Vishu mumbled to himself as he followed them into the building. His new life had definitely begun.

Made in the USA
Lexington, KY
17 September 2015